February's menu
BARONESSA GELATI
in Boston's North End

In addition to our regular flavors of Italian gelato, this month we are featuring:

- **A scrumptious taste of Italian-American beauty**

  Convent-bred Colleen Barone is full of sugar and spice and everything nice…except for a naughty twelve-year obsession with the college sweetheart she would never forget.

- **A supersized serving of Irish charm**

  Self-made tycoon Gavin O'Sullivan has overcome poverty, a tough neighborhood and a dysfunctional family, but can he ever fill the huge hole that Colleen Barone left in his heart?

- **An unexpected mix of flavors**

  The fortunes of the Barone family have been more sweet than bitter, leading many to doubt the validity of the family's Valentine's Day curse. But when the introduction of their newest ice cream flavor—passion fruit—is sabotaged on V-Day, the clan rallies to turn down the heat of bad publicity and salvage their company's reputation. Perhaps there is something to that curse after all….

Buon appetito!

Dear Reader,

Revel in the month with a special day devoted to
L-O-V-E by enjoying six passionate, powerful and
provocative romances from Silhouette Desire.

Learn the secret of the Barone family's Valentine's Day
curse, in *Sleeping Beauty's Billionaire* (#1489) by
Caroline Cross, the second of twelve titles in the continuity
series DYNASTIES: THE BARONES—the saga of an elite
clan, caught in a web of danger, deceit…and desire.

In *Kiss Me, Cowboy!* (#1490) by Maureen Child, a delicious
baker feeds the desire of a marriage-wary rancher. And
passion flares when a detective and a socialite undertake a
cross–country quest, in *That Blackhawk Bride* (#1491), the
most recent installment of Barbara McCauley's popular
SECRETS! miniseries.

A no-nonsense vet captures the attention of a royal bent
on seduction, in *Charming the Prince* (#1492), the newest
"fiery tale" by Laura Wright. In Meagan McKinney's latest
MATCHED IN MONTANA title, *Plain Jane & the Hotshot*
(#1493), a shy music teacher and a daredevil fireman
make perfect harmony. And a California businessman finds
himself longing for his girl Friday every day of the week, in
At the Tycoon's Command (#1494) by Shawna Delacorte.

Celebrate Valentine's Day by reading all six of the steamy
new love stories from Silhouette Desire this month.

Enjoy!

Joan Marlow Golan

Joan Marlow Golan
Senior Editor, Silhouette Desire

Please address questions and book requests to:
Silhouette Reader Service
U.S.: 3010 Walden Ave., P.O. Box 1325, Buffalo, NY 14269
Canadian: P.O. Box 609, Fort Erie, Ont. L2A 5X3

Sleeping Beauty's Billionaire
CAROLINE CROSS

Published by Silhouette Books

America's Publisher of Contemporary Romance

Special thanks and acknowledgment are given to Caroline Cross for her contribution to the DYNASTIES: THE BARONES series.

 SILHOUETTE BOOKS

ISBN 0-373-76489-8

SLEEPING BEAUTY'S BILLIONAIRE

Copyright © 2003 by Harlequin Books S.A.

This edition published by arrangement with Harlequin Books S.A.

® and TM are trademarks of Harlequin Books S.A., used under license. Trademarks indicated with ® are registered in the United States Patent and Trademark Office, the Canadian Trade Marks Office and in other countries.

Visit Silhouette at www.eHarlequin.com

Printed in U.S.A.

Books by Caroline Cross

Silhouette Desire

Dangerous #810
Rafferty's Angel #851
Truth or Dare #910
Operation Mommy #939
Gavin's Child #1013
The Baby Blizzard #1079
The Notorious Groom #1143
The Paternity Factor #1173
Cinderella's Tycoon #1238
The Rancher and the Nanny #1298
Husband—or Enemy? #1330
The Sheikh Takes a Bride #1424
Sleeping Beauty's Billionaire #1489

CAROLINE CROSS

always loved to read, but it wasn't until she discovered romance that she felt compelled to write, fascinated by the chance to explore the positive power of love in people's lives. She grew up in Yakima, Washington, the "Apple Capital of the World," attended the University of Puget Sound and now lives outside Seattle, where she (tries to) work at home despite the chaos created by two telephone-addicted teenage daughters and a husband with a fondness for home-improvement projects. Pleased to have recently been #1 on a national bestseller list, she was thrilled to win the 1999 Romance Writers of America RITA® Award for Best Short Contemporary Novel and to have been called "one of the best" writers of romance today by *Romantic Times*. Caroline believes in writing from the heart—and having a good brainstorming partner. She loves hearing from readers and can be reached at P.O. Box 47375, Seattle, Washington 98146. Please include a SASE for reply.

DYNASTIES: THE BARONES

Meet the Barones of Boston—
an elite clan caught in a web of danger, deceit…and desire!

Who's Who in
SLEEPING BEAUTY'S BILLIONAIRE

Gavin O'Sullivan—As owner of a luxury hotel chain, he was used to handling megadeals, beautiful women and a jet-set lifestyle. But Gavin never got used to the heartbreak he suffered because of the supposed snobbery of a Barone beauty.

Colleen Barone—Seven years as a nun and her work as a high school counselor couldn't erase the feelings Colleen still harbored for her college sweetheart. One look into his bedroom-brown eyes and she was again twenty…and in love with Gavin.

Carlo and Moira Barone—They've always wanted only the best for their brood, but when it comes to matters of the heart, Mama and Papa Barone are still learning that "the heart has reasons that Reason doesn't know."

One

"Hey, Colly, what's the matter? Why're you stopping?"

Colleen Barone only dimly registered her second cousin Matthew's inquiries. The nine-year-old's voice seemed far away as, her feet rooted in place, she stared transfixed at the tall, black-haired man who had just entered the reception hall.

Gavin O'Sullivan. Even among the throng of notable guests helping to celebrate her brother Nick's wedding—and so far she'd seen four U.S. senators, the current governor of Massachusetts and two of his predecessors, a bushel of Fortune 500 CEOs and a smattering of Hollywood movie stars—he stood out. And while Colleen wished it was merely because of his chiseled good looks or the impeccable tailoring of his expensive black suit, she knew better. There was simply something about the aloof way he held himself, the serious line of his sensual mouth, the reserve in his coffee-colored eyes, that set him apart.

But then, that was Gavin. Always so intense, so unpredictable, so alone.

Of course, there'd been a handful of brief exceptions to the latter. Once upon a time, for the three years they'd played soccer together at Madison Prep, he and Nick had been best friends. And then later, during her second year of college and his last, he and Colleen had shared for a little while what could only be called magic.

An ache, brief but savage, squeezed her heart. It had been twelve years since their last meeting, and the relationship had ended badly. Yet suddenly she longed to cross the space separating them, slip her hand into Gavin's and say something to make him smile.

If only it was that easy...

"Colleen!" Matthew's earnest voice coupled with his sharp tug on her hand jerked her back to reality.

Tearing her gaze from the man across the room, she looked down at her young companion. "What?"

He rolled his eyes. "I'm hungry, remember?"

As if someone had hit a switch, the totality of the reception hall snapped into focus for her. She heard the band playing, registered the noisy, shifting presence of the hundreds of guests, saw the impatience on her young relative's face. "Oh, Mattie, I'm sorry. Of course you are." Pushing away an edge of dismay— just how long had she been staring at Gavin, anyway?—she summoned a smile. "Lead the way."

"All *right*." His equanimity restored, the youngster tightened his grip on her hand and set off like a tugboat at full throttle. He chugged steadily past clumps of chatting guests and skillfully avoided knots of family members, not stopping until they finally arrived at the buffet, a vast spread laid out over a river of tabletops covered with crisp white linen.

The boy's gaze darted from the steaming casseroles to the heaps of Italian meat sliced paper thin, from stacks of golden calzones to platters of strawberries dipped in pale chocolate. He exhaled with gusty appreciation. "Wow."

Wow was right. In her usual over-the-top fashion, Colleen's mother, Moira, had made certain there was enough food on hand to feed all of Boston. Yet Colleen, who'd typically forgotten to eat that day and had been ravenous only a few minutes earlier, realized she no longer had an appetite.

The reason was obvious, and she felt a prick of annoyance at herself. Not that she intended to let on. Although Matthew probably wouldn't care, she refused to allow Gavin's unexpected presence to affect her behavior. After all, the time they'd been together had happened many years ago; neither of them was the person they'd been.

She knew she wasn't. After a difficult, painful struggle she'd learned to accept herself. She'd carved out a life rich with friends and a job where she felt she made a difference. And though there were times she was lonely and she still had her share of doubts and fears, frustrations and longings—life after all, was a constant and ever-changing challenge—in the ways that mattered most she was at peace for the first time ever.

So quit acting like a drama queen and eat, her practical side chided. Squaring her shoulders, she handed Matthew a gold-banded china plate, then took one for herself. "It looks good, doesn't it?" she said as she began serving them.

"Oh, yeah."

Thirty-five minutes and one return to the buffet line later, Matthew leaned back and exhaled in satisfaction. "That was really, really scrumpdillyitious," he announced.

Her lips quirked. "Yes, it was." Which was perfectly true as applied to the pathetically small amount she'd managed to get down. She set down her fork, grateful she could finally quit rearranging what was left on her plate.

Matt started to wipe the back of his hand

across his mouth, then apparently thought better of it as she raised an eyebrow at him. Sighing, he took a cursory swipe of his face with his napkin, tossed the linen square on the table and idly began to swing one leg.

He was silent for what was for him an uncharacteristically long moment. "Colleen?"

"Hmm?"

"Do you feel okay?"

She glanced over at him in surprise. "Sure."

"You're not mad at me or something?"

"Of course not. Why would you think that?"

He stared with sudden fascination at a spot of Alfredo sauce he'd dripped on the tablecloth and gave a slight, one-shouldered shrug. "I dunno. It's just…you're sort of quiet. For you. And you didn't eat very much, either. And earlier, when we were coming to get our food and then you stopped, you got a real funny look on your face. Kind of like Jordan Crenshaw did when I dared him to eat a dead frog."

"Gosh." Ignoring a concern that her earlier turmoil had been so apparent, she deliberately made her voice light. "And here I thought I was looking pretty good today."

Matt's head jerked up. "Oh, yeah! You do! For a girl. That is…" Flustered, he broke off. Heat stained his cheeks, but at least he was looking at her now, even if his expression was far too earnest. "It's just…I mean…it's just that usually you don't act like other grown-ups."

She'd certainly heard that before. Only normally it was from people her own age. "Ah." What the heck. She might as well take the plunge. "In what way?"

"Well…" He cocked his head, considering. "You really listen to me when we talk. And you never make me feel like you'd rather be somewhere else, with somebody else."

She blinked, gratified.

"And you don't act like you're smarter than me just because you're old."

That certainly put things in perspective; she swallowed a sudden bubble of laughter and did her best to look solemn. "Gee, maybe you'd better find me a cane. I wouldn't want to topple over when I stand up and fall in the punch bowl and embarrass us both."

For half a second the boy looked horrified. And then he realized she was kidding, and his eyes took on an impish gleam. "Naw. You're not *that* old." He did his best to match her deadpan delivery. "But if you were gonna fall down, we're a lot closer to the wedding cake. Now, that'd be really cool."

"Matthew!" Her protest was ruined by her sputter of laughter. "No wonder your mom says you're a menace."

He looked inordinately pleased. "Really? She said that?"

"I'm afraid so."

Before she could add that her cousin Janice had then said how crazy she was about the little rascal, his gaze settled on something behind her and he straightened like a bird dog who'd spotted a covey of quail. "Hey, it's Jeremy and Sean!" Like Matt, the two boys were distant cousins from Colleen's mother's side of the family and had recently become objects of Matt's veneration by virtue of having birthdays and officially becoming teenagers. "Can I go say hi?"

"Of course."

She didn't have to tell him twice. He shot

to his feet and disappeared almost before she gave her consent.

Fondly Colleen watched him go, relieved when the older boys welcomed him warmly. Looking away as a waiter approached, she declined an offer of champagne, taking a sip of her water, instead, as the young man quickly cleared away her and Matthew's plates.

The reception really had turned out to be a lovely affair, she reflected. A few tables away her brother Joseph was involved in an intense conversation with Uncle Paul, while her younger sisters, Rita, Gina and Maria, stood clustered together near the buffet, hands gesturing and faces alight as they chatted with one another.

Out on the dance floor, Nick glided into view, his arms securely cradling his bride, Gail. Hands clasped, heads together, the two were engrossed in each other. Colleen felt a wash of pleasure at their obvious happiness. Before meeting Gail, Nick hadn't had the easiest time when it came to love and romance.

A tendency that seemed to run in the family, she mused as she found herself searching the crowd for Gavin's black hair and broad shoulders. Assuring herself the sudden hollow feeling in the pit of her stomach was relief rather than disappointment when he was nowhere to be seen, she brushed a crumb off the table and told herself firmly she'd played hooky long enough.

At the very least, she should go check on "the aunts"—the contingent of widowed, black-clad, elderly ladies all gathered together at one big table like a flock of crows. Or, if she really wanted to feel virtuous, she could always seek out her mother....

Quit that, Colleen. Swallowing a sigh—was she ever going to outgrow the irreverent streak that too often got her in trouble?—she pushed back her chair, stood, squared her shoulders and turned.

And found herself gazing straight into the unsmiling face of Gavin O'Sullivan.

It wasn't fair. Twelve years, and she looked exactly the same, Gavin thought grimly. Dainty. Delicate. A doe-eyed waif with flawless skin and the hint of a dimple in one soft cheek.

The only thing different was her hair. Gone

was the ebony sheaf that had once fallen in a silken tumble to her waist. In its place was a cropped, tousled cap that somehow made her neck seem more fragile, her straight little nose finer, her densely lashed blue eyes even bigger.

Not that he gave a rip. His sole reason for seeking her out was to get this encounter over with. He'd come to celebrate Nick's wedding, and he was damned if he was going to spend his time worrying about inadvertently bumping into her. Better by far to take the direct route, where he called the shots. Just to make sure that she or anyone else who might recall they'd once had a thing for each other would be absolutely clear he was long over her.

He summoned the polite, impersonal smile that was his stock-in-trade in social settings. "Hello, Colleen. It's been a long time."

For a second longer than was strictly polite her gaze remained riveted on his face. Then she seemed to catch herself and, as if recalling her manners, smiled and said, "Gavin. How nice to see you."

He'd forgotten what an appealing voice she had. Soft, a little husky, with a warmth that wrapped gently around whomever she was addressing like a well-worn flannel blanket. Too bad it was merely part of her act.

"Does Nick know you're here?" For an instant she sounded almost nervous, but then her voice evened out and he knew he must've imagined it. "Have you talked to him yet?"

What did she think? That he was still some ill-mannered inner-city kid who didn't know how to behave at a fancy wedding? "Sure. I saw him when I went through the reception line."

"Oh. He must be so pleased that you came."

He shrugged. "I wouldn't know about that. I do know I've enjoyed seeing him again."

"Of course." Although her pleasant expression didn't alter, a shadow darkened her eyes, and he knew she'd heard the slight but deliberate emphasis he'd put on *him*.

He felt a flick of satisfaction.

In the next instant he asked himself what in hell he was doing. It had been years since their breakup, damn it. And while being dumped by Colleen had been hard at the time, it was nothing compared to some of the other things he'd endured in his life. Losing a girlfriend just wasn't in the same category as being raised, if it could be called that, by an alcoholic single mother in one of Boston's toughest neighborhoods. Or getting himself not just through high school but also through college. Or even having to learn about art and culture later in life because such "civilized" things had taken a back seat to survival when he'd been younger.

What was more, the intervening years had been good to him. He'd transformed himself from a dirt-poor charity case to a rich, respected, successful hotelier whose extensive holdings provided jobs for hundreds of people.

And he certainly hadn't lived like a monk while he'd done it. In the time since he and Colleen had parted ways, he'd dated his share of women. Most of them, at least lately, tended to be either up-and-coming actresses, members of what was left of European aristocracy or international supermodels.

So maybe he should try not to act like some petulant kid; maybe he could even see his way clear to give little Ms. Barone a break. After all, there was a chance, slight though it was, that he might not be where he was if she hadn't chosen to stomp on his heart all those years ago.

"Dance with me," he said abruptly as the band struck up a new song.

Her eyes widened and for a second something that looked almost like panic gleamed in their sapphire depths. "I beg your pardon?"

What the hell. So he wasn't a saint; but what could it hurt if by acting like an adult he also gave her a taste of what she'd thrown away? He deliberately softened his voice. "Dance with me, Colleen. Please?"

She hesitated another instant, then her face smoothed out as she apparently decided he was now upwardly mobile enough to warrant her attention. "All right." Flashing him a quick smile he might have deemed shyly beguiling had she been anyone else, she headed for the dance floor.

He fell in behind her. Refusing to debate the wisdom of what he was doing, he forced himself to concentrate on the slow but catchy beat of the love song the band was crooning—and not the supple line of her back. By the time they reached the outer circle of dancers, he was ready. Taking Colleen's slender hand in his much bigger one, he slid his other palm to rest on the small of her back, pressed her close and led her into the dance.

Given the awkwardness of their reunion, the acrimony of their former parting and the disparity of their heights, their coming together should have been more than a little graceless.

Instead, from their first step they were perfectly matched, melting together in a rhythm that was as instinctive as breathing—or sex.

"Oh, my," Colleen murmured.

"What?" Even to his own ears, he sounded a little terse, but then, the last thing he'd expected was the pleasure that was currently sizzling along his nerves.

"I'd just...forgotten." She raised her chin and met his gaze, an unexpected and oddly self-effacing expression on her fine-boned face. "It's been a long time since I danced. I'd forgotten how nice it is."

Nice? That was the last word he'd use to describe the awareness tingling through him like ungrounded electricity. "Yeah. Right."

She cocked her head. "When did you finally learn?"

"What?"

"To dance. As I recall, you didn't... before."

Now there was a diplomatic choice of words. For a second he was tempted to make her squirm, to politely inquire, "Do you mean before you discarded me like yesterday's newspaper, with no more explanation than we didn't suit and you didn't want to see me anymore?"

But then he reminded himself of his decision not to be petty. Which was no doubt good since a second later the band launched into a complicated instrumental riff that sounded as if it might keep them together longer than he'd been counting on.

What wasn't good was the discovery that he wanted in the worst way to look away from Colleen's gaze so that he could bury his face in the delicate curve where her neck met her shoulder and drink her in, inhale her scent, taste her skin, savor the flavor of her on his tongue. Just like that, any sort of distraction, including conversation, seemed like a damn good idea. "I took lessons. Arthur Murray."

"You're kidding." She couldn't hide her amazement.

Annoyed and not sure why, except that it pissed him off royally to be lusting after a woman he didn't like, he retorted, "I'm dead serious. Elliot insisted."

"Elliot?"

Terrific. If ever there was a subject he didn't care to discuss with her, this was it. "Elliot Sutherland," he said repressively. Determined to distract her long enough to retake control of the conversation, not to mention his treacherous body, he executed a complicated series of steps.

She followed effortlessly, not missing a beat. "I apologize if I ought to recognize his name, but I don't," she said easily. "Is he a friend?"

"Yes."

She continued to look at him, the picture of interest—and endless patience. Clearly, she wasn't going to drop the subject.

"Elliot was my boss." *And the closest thing to a father I ever had.* Not that she needed to know that. Or would care if she did. "He owned the Independence Hotel downtown and he gave me my first real job in the business." Not to mention the mantle of his chosen successor. Thanks to Elliot's having noticed Gavin's savvy business mind and solid work ethic, today Gavin stood before Colleen a wealthy hotelier with five-star lodgings all over the country. He'd done his best to make Elliot proud, adding hotels to the chain over the years. But he never lost sight of his humble beginnings.

"Elliot's and my backgrounds were similar, so he took an interest in me. In addition to teaching me everything I know about business, he also insisted I learn some other things."

"Like how to dance?" she said softly.

"Yeah. Like how to dance. And dress. And use the right fork and choose the right wine at dinner." Try as he might, he just couldn't keep the trace of sarcasm out of his voice. "Hell, he even made sure I'd know how to behave at a big society wedding."

She flinched, just as he'd intended. Yet rather than experiencing satisfaction, he felt more than a little ashamed of himself. Colleen might be a spoiled, social-conscious snob, but he was no bully. Nor was he likely to make her regret giving him up if he kept behaving like a callow jerk still smarting from a long-ago rejection.

Which he wasn't. He'd gotten past that a long time ago.

Yeah? Then prove it. See if you can't locate a little of the Irish charm Clarice and Caroline and Angelina and the rest of your dates are always prattling on about.

He drew Colleen slightly closer. Ignoring the treacherous leap of his pulse, he swung her around and reversed direction as they reached the edge of the dance floor. "So what about you?" he inquired, doing his best to sound mildly curious and nothing more. "Did you get your teaching degree?" Given her chic little haircut and stylish suit, it was easy to imagine her teaching French or Nineteenth-Century Romantic Poets to a giggly group of teenage girls at some posh private school.

Some of the tension left her body. "Yes, I did."

"So what are you doing these days?"

"I run a counseling program for gifted but at-risk kids at Jefferson High."

He missed a step. "You *what?*" Surely he hadn't heard her right.

Her voice held a totally unexpected hint of wryness. "Don't look so horrified."

"I'm not. Just…surprised." That was putting it mildly. Jefferson was his alma mater, a tough school in an even tougher neighborhood. Given Colleen's privileged, sheltered, parochial-school background, he would've thought she was joking if not for the calm, steady way she was gazing up at him. "When did you start?" Even if she was being serious, surely this had to be something recent, some sort of fleeting, poor-little-rich-girl scheme to help the needy and downtrodden.

"This is my third year."

For a moment he was so stunned he couldn't think what to say. "And your family—your parents—are all right with it?" he finally managed. He simply couldn't imagine the fashionable Moira Barone allowing such a thing.

Colleen gave a slight shrug. "They're not wild about it. But then, they were so overwrought when I decided to leave the order that they consider my subsequent errors in judgment these last three years minor in comparison."

Her voice was so matter-of-fact it took a moment for her words to sink in. "You left... What order? What the hell are you talking about?"

All solemn blue eyes, she looked up at him. "I'm sorry. I just assumed you knew."

"Knew what?"

"After we broke up...and after college, I joined the Sisters of Charity. For seven years I was a nun."

Two

"Hey, lady." The cabbie turned to give Colleen a quick, questioning glance over his shoulder, then twisted back around to peer through the windshield at the street ahead. "You sure you gave me the right address?"

Jarred from her thoughts, she contemplated the back of the man's balding head and told herself to focus. "Yes, of course. Why do you ask?"

He snorted with disbelief. "You're kiddin', right?" He lifted a hand off the wheel and gestured at the surrounding area. "Take a look around. In case you haven't noticed, this ain't exactly Beacon Hill."

She dutifully turned her head although she already knew what she'd find outside. With each block they passed, the sidewalks grew narrower, the store signs less refined, the building facades dingier. More and more steel and iron grills secured by chains and padlocks protected businesses; more upper-story windows were barred.

Wryly she conceded the cabbie had a point; the area didn't bear the slightest resemblance to either Beacon Hill or the upscale neighborhood where Nick and Gail's wedding reception had just been held.

Yet as she noted the eclectic mix of people on the street, some standing and chatting, some coming and going from various bars, cafés and delis, some clearly intent on getting somewhere else, she felt a distinct fondness for the area. It might not be squeaky clean nor even particularly attractive, but it was very much alive, with no pretensions. It was also home.

"You're right. It's not Beacon Hill. But we

are in the right place. My street is the third one after the next light. When you reach it, go right, and my building is a few blocks down, just past a small park.''

The man parted his lips as if to make yet another disapproving observation, then seemed to think better of it. He shrugged. ''Whatever you say.''

Colleen swallowed a smile, suspecting his sudden lack of opinion had more to do with the sizable tip he'd been promised by her father than a sudden appreciation of the neighborhood. Carlo Barone had not only insisted on calling her a cab, but had told the driver he'd get an extra twenty if he saw her to her door. Then, ignoring her protests, he'd pressed a wad of bills into her palm as he'd handed her into the back seat, given her a tender kiss on the cheek and told her to take care of herself and ''not be such a stranger.''

Dear Papa. They'd always had a special bond, no doubt in part because she'd been the only girl among the four boys in the family until she'd been five and Gina had arrived. Even so, it had been a distinct shock when she'd eventually come to realize that her decision to join the Sisters of Charity had sprung not from a true vocation on her part, but from a desire to fulfill her father's long-held dream for her and, to a lesser extent, to please her mother.

And? prompted the gentle voice of her conscience.

She shifted on the vinyl-covered seat. Ever since she'd admitted to herself—and God—that she wasn't meant to be a nun, she'd vowed she'd always be honest with Him and herself, no matter how difficult or humbling.

So quit avoiding the other reason you knew you weren't meant to stay in the order. Admit that despite the passage of time, you never completely quit having feelings for Gavin. That for all these years, a part of you has continued to long for him—the sound of his voice, the scent of his skin, the warmth of his touch…his presence in your life.

The shudder of pleasure she hadn't allowed herself at the time swept through her now as she recalled how it had felt to be held in his arms on the dance floor tonight. She squeezed her eyes shut, thanking the Almighty for lending her the strength to appear composed, to keep the conversation light, to not make a fool of herself and blurt out to Gavin that she'd never stopped missing him.

She also thanked God for helping her keep her chin up when, moments after telling Gavin she'd spent most of the past decade as a nun, he'd fled. Or close enough. Conveniently for him, the music had ended a few seconds after her revelation. Murmuring an uninflected, "I see," he'd glanced at his watch and grimaced. "I'm sorry to be abrupt, but there's a phone call I need to make." He'd looked up, flashing her a duplicate of the polite, impersonal smile with which he'd first greeted her. "It's been nice seeing you, Colleen. Thanks for the dance." Then he'd turned and walked away, leaving her standing alone on the dance floor.

"Jeez, lady, is that what you mean by a park?"

The cabbie's incredulous question put a merciful end to Colleen's recollections. She snapped her eyes open, grasping at the chance to concentrate on the present, even though she knew she was only postponing the inevitable. Like it or not, she was going to have to deal with the caldron of feelings her encounter with Gavin had stirred up.

But not yet. "Pardon me?"

"I said, is that the park you were talking about?" He waved at the dark patch of ground that stretched between the lighted brownstones like a dark gap between a row of pearly teeth.

"Yes, it is."

"Huh." He met her gaze in the rearview mirror as he slowed the taxi and pulled to the curb. "Where I live, we'd call that a vacant lot."

She did her best to look serene. "Everyone is entitled to his opinion." Besides, she hadn't a doubt that once the bulbs she'd planted came up this spring and she added a few trees, a couple of birdbaths and a bench or two, it would look much more parklike, something the cabdriver couldn't possibly be expected to know.

"Yeah, that's true. That's why we live in a democracy."

Frowning, she realized someone was sitting on her front stairs. "Actually, the United States is a republic," she said automatically as she reached for the door handle. "What do I owe you?"

The man rattled off the amount on the meter. "Plus two sawbucks for—"

"Seeing me to the stoop. I remember. But it's really not necessary as it appears I have company. Here's the fare—" she leaned forward and thrust the money at him "—and your twenty, plus an extra five for being so nice." Flashing him a bright smile, she scooted out onto the sidewalk. "Have a lovely night."

"But your old man said—"

"Good night," she said, firmly shutting the door. Then, taking a deep, calming breath and composing herself, she turned just as the shadowy figure climbed to its feet, revealed by the streetlight to be a tall, dark-haired teenager. "Brett? Is that you?"

Hunching his shoulders, the youngster thrust his hands into his front pants pockets. "Hey, Ms. Barone."

Muscles she hadn't known she'd tensed slowly relaxed, while questions crowded her tongue. Oh, dear. Why was he here at this hour? Had he been in a fight? Was he hurt?

In trouble with the law? Had he had another argument with his mother? Or had the woman kicked him out again because she was "entertaining" one of her boyfriends?

Yet as she crossed the sidewalk and started up the steps, Colleen knew better than to ask, at least not right away. Of all the students she counseled at Jefferson High, Brett Maguiness was both the most talented and academically gifted—and the most private.

He was also her favorite, although she was careful not to show it. In her heart of hearts, however, she couldn't deny that there was something about the moody youngster with the guarded eyes that had pulled at her from the instant they'd met at the start of the previous school year.

"Goodness, but it's cold out here." With a shiver that wasn't feigned, she stepped past him to unlock the door to the vestibule. "Have you been waiting long?"

He hiked his shoulders in the nonchalant shrug she considered his trademark. "Awhile."

She let it go, since it wasn't really important. "Well, what do you say we get inside where it's warmer?'' She pushed the outer door open and proceeded to the inner one, trusting him to follow.

Moments later they were walking down the short hallway to her ground-floor apartment. The sound of a violin concerto drifted sweetly from the floor above. Brett made a vaguely rude noise. ''Sounds like the geezer's having his usual wild night.''

''The geezer has a name, and you know it,'' she said mildly. ''It's Mr. Crypinski.'' The older man, a retired transit worker, owned the converted brownstone and lived on the second floor.

''Huh. Creepinski is more like it.''

She glanced at the teenager, startled by the rancor in his voice. ''Did something happen between you two?''

''Nothing important.''

''Then you won't mind telling me about it.''

He rolled his eyes. ''Fine. If you gotta know, I buzzed him and asked if he'd let me in so I could wait for you in the vestibule. And you know what he said? He said that I might have you fooled but he knew a shiftless young thug when he saw one.''

"Oh, dear. I can't imagine..." Though gruff, her landlord had never been anything but kind toward her. Yet she also knew Brett well enough to know he never made things up. "I'll talk to him."

"No."

"Brett—"

"No. He's probably hoping you'll do just that so he can call me a wuss or something. So just forget it, all right?"

She considered an instant, then nodded. "Okay." She'd simply have to find a different way to approach the problem, she decided as she worked the locks on the front door and pushed it open. Switching on a light, she shed her coat and hung it and her purse on the brass wall rack. She turned, glad to be home in her very own space.

Not that there was a lot of it, she acknowledged. Like the lot it was built on, the converted brownstone was long and narrow front to back. Her portion of it consisted of the postage-size entry, with the bedroom, bathroom and utility room stretching down one side of the house, and the living room, kitchen and pantry down the other.

What it lacked in size, it made up for in character, however. The old wood floors had aged to a burnished, golden hue and the high plaster ceilings boasted ornate crown molding.

But Colleen's favorite feature was the bank of floor-to-ceiling windows at the far side of the living room. Her brother Joe might consider "all that glass a break-in just waiting to happen," but Colleen loved being able to look out on her small garden. Like the park next door, it wouldn't be long before the first crocuses began to appear, followed by the constantly changing tableau of blooming flowers, bushes and trees that would go on until the first fall freeze.

"Would you put the kettle on while I go change?" she asked Brett. She could hardly wait to shed her high heels and panty hose.

"Sure."

"Help yourself to a glass of milk or a soda. And there's some lasagna in the fridge if you're hungry."

"Who made it?"

Headed toward her bedroom, she stopped, turned and made a wry face at him. "My sister."

"Great."

Amused, she watched as he hurried toward the kitchen. Due to the brownstone's high ceilings and wide doorways, she could see him perfectly well as he turned on the light and yanked open the appliance door. "Someday my cooking's going to improve and you're going to be sorry for your attitude," she warned.

He straightened and turned, a casserole dish in one hand, a carton of milk in the other, and flashed her a grin. "I'm not holding my breath."

Even as she warmed at the sight of that rare, sunny smile, her stomach clenched. The brightly illuminated kitchen revealed what she hadn't seen before. The corner of the boy's right eye and the cheek below were bruised and puffy.

She parted her lips to ask what had happened, then clamped them shut. She and Brett had been down this road before during the past six months and she knew what to expect. At her very first question, his smile would vanish and the usual guarded look would come over his face. Next he'd claim that he'd run into a door, or something else equally as lame. Then he'd make an excuse to leave.

And if she reported, as she had the last two times, her suspicions that he'd tangled with one of his mother's boyfriends, he'd vanish. He'd go to ground on the streets, not showing up at school for weeks. And when he finally did return, he'd stick stubbornly to whatever story he'd told initially.

"Hmm." Somehow she managed a smile. "Well, don't say I didn't warn you." And with that she twisted around and slipped into her room. Shutting the door, she leaned back against it and allowed herself a sigh of frustration.

Darn it! How could she justify collecting a paycheck, much less live with herself, if she couldn't find a way to provide help when it was needed? Brett was such a good kid at heart, but if something in his life didn't change soon and for the better, there was a more than good chance she'd lose him. He already had two strikes against him—an absent father and an alcoholic mother. Add to that his tendency to keep things bottled up inside, and it was a recipe for disaster.

If only she could find—and convince him to accept—a good foster home. Or even provide him with a role model, someone to show him that real men didn't have to resort to violence to get their way, that he could rise above his beginnings if he stayed in school, applied himself and didn't give up.

Like a genie escaping a bottle, an image of Gavin popped into her mind. With absolute clarity, she recalled the warmth that had crept into his voice when he'd talked about the older man who'd helped him get started in the hotel business.

Transfixed, she wondered why she hadn't thought of it before. Of course! What Brett and the rest of her kids needed were mentors. People who came from similar backgrounds, who'd faced some of the same things they confronted every day and had succeeded, anyway. What's more, Gavin would be the absolutely perfect match for Brett.

She tried to push the idea away, but it wouldn't budge.

Yet lodged with it was the recollection of the coolness that had been in Gavin's voice when he'd spoken to her, the reserve with which he'd treated her, the hurried way he'd said goodbye the instant it was politely feasible. A dull ache blossomed in the region of her heart as she faced a truth she'd been trying to avoid for hours.

Whatever feelings he'd once had for her were dead. The best thing she could do for both of them was keep her distance so they could both get on with their lives.

And yet, if he could help Brett...

She instinctively glanced heavenward. "I don't know if this is part of Your plan for me, but I'm not making any promises," she warned Him, her feelings as tangled as a ball of yarn tossed into a roomful of kittens. "Except that I'll think about it."

For now that would have to be enough.

A nun.

Gavin stared unseeingly at the columns of January revenue figures laid out on his desk.

A *nun.* The word—and all it implied—had been rattling around in his head for the past four days, surfacing at odd moments to ruin his concentration.

And he was damned if he knew why. After

all, as he'd proved at Nick's wedding reception, Colleen meant nothing to him.

It was just… He didn't like the idea of anybody locking themselves away, wasting vital years of their life, in a convent. It was the twenty-first century, for God's sake. Women had choices. And though he'd never thought about it before now, it seemed pretty obvious that prior to making a commitment to the Church, a young woman like Colleen should be required to have some real life experience.

Oh yeah? Like what? Sleeping with you?

Terrific. On top of everything else, now he was being ambushed by his own mind—or what was left of it. Irritated, he slapped the report shut, shoved back his chair and climbed to his feet, then paced over to the large windows that overlooked the street forty stories below. A nerve ticked to life in his jaw.

Who would've thought that after all this time something as tame as dancing with Colleen would be enough to kick his hormones into overdrive? Much less that just thinking about her days later—the fragile hollow at the base of her throat, the slight weight of her hand in his, her faint but never forgotten lily-of-the-valley scent—could make his temperature rise and his skin feel tight?

Not him, that was for damned sure, he thought grimly. If you'd asked him a week ago what he thought about Colleen, he would have replied flatly, "I don't." And now he couldn't seem to get her out of his mind.

There was a soft rap on his door. "What?" he barked, impatiently shoving a hand through his hair.

His secretary poked her head in. "I'm sorry to bother you, but I buzzed the intercom and you didn't answer—"

"What is it, Carol?"

"A Ms. Barone is here to see you. She doesn't have an appointment, and I told her you were busy, but she asked me to tell you she only needed a few minutes."

For an instant he felt nonplussed, as if his thoughts had somehow conjured up Colleen. Then the moment passed and his normal pragmatism kicked in. Whatever the reason for her sudden appearance, seeing her again could only be a good thing. In the clear light of day, on his own turf, he'd no doubt be able to consign her to where she belonged—in the past.

He walked back to his desk and sat. "It's okay. Show her in."

Quickly masking her surprise, his secretary inclined her head. "You're the boss." She backed away, then returned moments later, ushered his visitor to a chair and discreetly departed.

Having learned the power of silence, Gavin took a good look at the woman who'd been in his thoughts far too much lately. Her finery of Saturday night was gone. Today she was casually dressed in low-heeled boots, slim-fitting black slacks and a fuzzy, pale peach turtleneck sweater. An inexpensive-looking black wool coat was folded over her arm, a small black satchel slung over her shoulder.

She looked great.

"Hi." Her smile was tentative. "I know I should have called, but—"

"What do you want, Colleen?" The words came out harsher than he intended, but he didn't care.

For a split second she appeared taken aback. Then she quickly gathered her composure. "I'd like to talk to you."

"About what?"

Perched on the edge of her chair, she laced her fingers together. "Actually, I have a favor to ask."

"I see." He didn't see at all. What could she possibly want from him? He couldn't think of a thing. Unless…

He thought again about their turn on the dance floor the other night. Hell, maybe he wasn't the only one who'd felt hot and bothered by their encounter. Maybe she'd experienced a similar rise in temperature and was interested in finally finishing what they'd started all those years ago—

"It's not for me, really, but for my kids. The ones from my school."

The prickle of anticipation he was feeling vanished, replaced by self-disgust. When, exactly, was he going to learn? Colleen hadn't wanted him when they were younger, and obviously nothing had changed.

He reached over, opened the appropriate desk drawer and pulled out his checkbook. Flipping it open, he picked up his pen and angled a hard look at her. "How much do you want?"

Her eyes widened. "Pardon me?"

He held her gaze. "I said, how much? You can spare me the pep talk about whatever project you want the money for or how great the kids are. Just give me the bottom line."

"Oh, dear. Obviously I'm not explaining myself very well. I don't want your money, Gavin. I want *you*." A faint flush rose in her baby-smooth cheeks as she appeared to realize what she'd just said. "That is, I want your time," she hastily clarified. "I'm putting together a mentoring program, and I need you."

She needed him? For all of ten seconds he felt the siren call of being wanted. Then his sanity kicked in. "No."

She went on as if he hadn't spoken. "I have a student, Brett Maguiness. He's smart, special, but he needs a man in his life, someone he can look up to, who's carved out his own success—"

"No." He'd be a bigger fool than he already was if he let a little flattery sway him. "I'll be glad to donate money if it'll help, but I can't spare the time." Not that he would if he could. It was entirely out of the question. The last thing he needed was involvement in an endeavor guaranteed to bring Colleen and him together on a regular basis. Not when by merely walking into a room she could make his libido attempt to hijack his brain.

"This is a boy on the brink," she continued. "He desperately needs someone like your Mr. Sutherland." Reaching across the desk, she touched gentle fingertips to the back of his tensed hand. "Please, Gavin."

Sex drive screaming, he looked into her dark blue eyes and for a moment felt as if he were drowning. Sternly he reminded himself she was not to be trusted, that the one other time he'd given in to temptation and allowed her close to him, she'd ripped out his heart.

It was a hell of a shock, then, when he opened his mouth to tell her to leave and, instead, heard himself say, "When would you want me to start?"

Three

He'd blown it.

Gavin angled a swift gaze sideways at Brett. The boy sat stiff and silent on the Porsche's sleek black leather seat, his face ever-so-slightly averted, his gaze fixed on the view outside with seeming fascination.

Given that they were traveling on a section of road surrounded by warehouses and that rain was pouring from the inky February sky in sheets, Gavin doubted the kid was admiring the scenery.

"Ugly night out," he commented, taking yet another stab at conversation.

"Uh-huh."

"The wind's coming out of the north. Maybe we'll get snow tonight."

Brett continued to look out the window. "Maybe."

And maybe I'll drop dead, which might give you something to talk about, if only briefly. With a frustrated shake of his head, Gavin considered the wet, shining pavement and tried to pinpoint the exact moment things had started to go sour.

How about the second you clapped eyes on Colleen again?

He shoved the renegade thought away. As much as he'd like to blame this on her, he couldn't. For starters, *he'd* approached her at Nick's reception. What's more, it had been *his* decision to let her into his office. And she sure as hell hadn't been holding a gun to his head when he'd opened his big mouth and agreed to this mentoring thing.

But at least he was consistent in his use of poor judgment. Take earlier tonight. When Colleen had shared some ideas with the adult volunteers who'd gathered at the high school on how best to break the ice with the kids they were mentoring, he'd blown off her words, convinced he didn't need her advice.

He'd been right, too. At first.

Though unmistakably wary at their initial introduction, Brett had relaxed a little when he'd seen that, unlike some of the other mentors who'd chosen to wear suits and ties, Gavin had dressed in jeans, a plain black sweater and a black leather jacket. And like any other red-blooded teenager, the boy had been enamored with Gavin's silver sports car the instant he'd laid eyes on it.

Not that he'd fallen all over himself oohing and ahhing or anything. Instead, with all the nonchalance of someone who rode in a $100,000 car every day, he'd yanked open the door, slung himself onto the glove-soft seat, taken in the custom-made burled-walnut dashboard with its polished steel dials and murmured, "Nice."

At the time, Gavin had found the kid's determined cool amusing. Now it didn't seem the least bit funny. On the contrary, it stood out as the high point of the evening. And it was his own damn fault. Colleen had advised him and the others to keep this first meeting simple, go someplace in the neighborhood for coffee and conversation, and let the youngster set the tone.

And what had he done? He'd taken Brett downtown to the Independence, given him a tour of the hotel, including the view from the penthouse he called home, then ushered him into the main dining room for a five-star dinner.

He had to give himself credit, though. Not for nothing was he known in the business world as a mind reader, as well as a tough negotiator. Once they were ensconced at his favorite table, it had taken him only fifteen or twenty minutes of conversation—with Brett's contribution consisting of half-a-dozen mumbled *yeahs* and *nos* accompanied by a handful of dismissive shrugs—to get the message.

When it came to mentoring, he sucked.

Now that it was too late, he could see that instead of showing the teen that where a man came from didn't matter as much as where he ended up, he'd yanked the kid out of his comfort zone, dragged him into foreign territory, then practically put him on display. And though it hadn't been his intent, he suspected he'd managed to look like a self-absorbed jerk in the process.

So? It didn't work. So what? Look at the upside. Now you can tell Colleen you gave it a shot and missed the target by a mile. You can say goodbye, adios, see you later.

There was only one problem with that. And it happened to be sitting beside him.

He tightened his grip on the steering wheel and took a left, headed for the westernmost Fort Point Channel bridge and Jefferson Heights.

The truth was he wanted a shot at making a difference in this kid's life. And not because of Colleen, but despite her—something he'd realized once she'd left the other day and he'd had time to think about his sudden decision to volunteer.

For as long as he could remember, work had dominated his life. Recently, however, though no less busy, he'd been feeling restless, out of sorts, vaguely dissatisfied with his life. He didn't have any family obligations—his mother had partied herself into an early grave years ago, he'd never known who his father was, and last summer Elliot had finally lost his long battle with cancer. Plus, he'd experienced enough real hardship in his life to know he currently had nothing to bitch about. Given that, the answer to his dissatisfaction had seemed obvious: do something for somebody else. To that end, recently he'd been considering getting involved in a number of good causes, from the Make-A-Wish Foundation to Habitat for Humanity.

Instead, he'd chosen to take on a tough-as-nails teenager.

He slowed the car slightly at the approach to the bridge, then slowed even more as a strong gust of wind buffeted the bridge and the brake lights on the car in front of him flashed. Narrowing his eyes, he told himself to concentrate on his driving, but he couldn't entirely block out the voice in his head.

The one saying, *Yeah? And the instant things don't go your way, you decide to blow out? Get real, O'Sullivan.*

Well, hell. With sudden decisiveness, he accelerated as the car left the bridge and

switched lanes. He passed through the next series of traffic lights, then took a right.

Brett shifted to look at him. "You turned
too soon. I told you to drop me on Market.
You *do* know where Market is, don't you?"

"It's been a while, but yeah, I do," Gavin
replied evenly. He sensed the kid's impatience, but he deliberately didn't say anything
more.

A good thirty seconds passed. Finally the
boy gave vent to his exasperation with a loud
sigh. "So? Where are we going?"

"There's something I want to show you."

Suspicion instantly colored the young voice.
"What?"

"Relax, kid. I've got my faults, but whatever you're thinking isn't one of them. And
before you say anything..." He raised a hand
to forestall the attitude he could see building
on the youth's face. "—I don't expect you to
trust me—" *not yet, anyway* "—but you
ought to have a little more faith in Ms. Barone."

"I do," the boy said defensively.

"Then relax, okay?" Frowning, he stared
hard at the dimly lit street, trying to get his

bearings. He thought for a moment he'd passed his destination, then saw a second later that he hadn't.

The property at 121 Calhoon Street hadn't changed much. The brick facade was still dingy and crumbling, just the way he remembered. All the front windows were boarded up, with only a glimmer of light leaking here and there to suggest that anyone actually lived inside. Black plastic trash bags spilling garbage were heaped around the entrance and piled on the crumbling sidewalk, where a few scraggly weeds poked up in defiance of the winter weather. As a final touch, a soiled mattress shedding its stuffing rested at a crazy angle against the stoop, impaled on the finial of the one iron balustrade still standing.

Gavin brought the Porsche to a stop, staring at the building he'd deliberately avoided for more than sixteen years. He braced, waiting for the familiar sense of shame and disgust; instead, all he felt was a sort of sadness for the boy he'd been.

The discovery was oddly liberating. "See that?" he said to Brett, nodding at the neglected building.

"Yeah."

"When I wasn't in emergency foster care, that's where I lived the last few months of high school. It's pretty typical of the sort of places my mom and I called home over the years."

Lips pursed, the boy considered a moment, then turned to Gavin and regarded him through narrowed eyes. "So? You don't live there anymore."

Gavin met his gaze straight on. "And nobody's more thankful than I am for that. But the point is, I do have some idea of where you're coming from. I realize we haven't gotten off to the best start, but I'd like another chance."

Brett turned his gaze back to the crumbling tenement. He was silent so long and his expression was so blank that Gavin was on the verge of losing hope by the time the boy finally gave an elaborate shrug. "Sure. Why not?"

Relief flooded Gavin, but he knew better than to show it. "Good." Doing his best to match the kid's offhand manner, he put the car into gear and headed back the way they'd come. He turned onto Central and within a few minutes had reached Market Street. Pulling into the first open spot he saw along the curb, he let the engine idle and glanced over at Brett. "You like basketball?"

"It's okay."

"Would you be interested in going to Saturday's Celtics game?" Tied for the lead in the Atlantic Division, the Celtics were playing the Knicks, their longtime rival. The game had been sold out for weeks.

True to form, the boy did his best to look blasé, but there was a spark of interest in his eyes he couldn't disguise. "Yeah, I guess."

"Okay. I'll check the game time and give you a call, all right?"

"Sure." Brett shoved open the car door and climbed out onto the sidewalk. He took a step, then hesitated. Squaring his shoulders, he turned and ducked his head so he and Gavin were eye level. "I don't…that is, well, thanks. For dinner and—" he made a vague, all-encompassing gesture "—stuff."

"No problem."

A sudden gust of wind blew the teen's dark hair into his eyes and he impatiently shoved it away. "And, uh, if you've gotta plan ahead or something, I guess it'd be okay if you picked me up on Saturday. If you want."

The admission amounted to a display of trust, and Gavin knew it. Encouraged, but aware that to show it would be a major breach of 'hood etiquette, he merely nodded. "Sure."

"Okay, then. I'll see you." With a brief nod, Brett straightened and walked away.

Gavin watched him go, filled with satisfaction. Hell, who was he kidding? If he'd been twenty years younger, he'd have been tempted to punch the air with his fist.

Instead, he reached for his cell phone, only to stop midmotion as reality struck. Just who did he think he was going to call? He couldn't think of a single one of his high-powered friends who'd understand what he was feeling. Particularly when he had no intention of discussing what passed as his childhood with them.

He shook his head at his own foolishness, telling himself to grow up and forget this uncharacteristic urge he had to share what had just transpired. After all, it wasn't as if he had any options. Did he?

It was an unfortunate question, he realized the instant a certain female image sprang to mind. Scowling, he put the Porsche in gear, waited for a break in traffic, then pulled into it.

No way was he going *there*.

Was he?

The harsh burr of the doorbell gave Colleen a start.

Stretched out on the faded imitation-Persian rug before the fireplace in her living room, she brought her head up at the urgent sound.

Outside, the wind was putting on a show, perfectly still one second, tossing raindrops against the windowpane and plucking fretfully at the sashes the next.

Inside, everything was peaceful, herself included. If the phone calls she'd received in the past few hours from various adults and kids were any indication, the mentoring program was going to be a success.

She'd love to take credit, but she knew who was truly responsible, and was thankful to Him for His guidance and for helping her make wise matches. Not to mention—she gave a slight shudder as a spate of sleet tattooed the courtyard—seeing fit to hold back the storm until after the meeting.

The buzzer sounded again, and with a resigned sigh she rose to her feet. Her intercom had died a few weeks ago, and she kept forgetting to tell Mr. Crypinski. Hugging her arms to herself, she stepped out of her cozy apartment and into the chilly hall, catching a distorted glimpse of dark hair and the back of a leather jacket through the mottled glass of the entry sidelight. With a pinch of concern, she hurried down the hall and yanked open the door. "Brett?"

Her visitor swiveled around. "No."

"Gavin!" How could she not have known? He was taller than Brett. Taller, broader of shoulder, narrower of hip. And in a category of his own when it came to being intensely, maturely, blatantly male. "What are you doing here? Is everything all right?"

"Yeah. I just thought I'd...report in."

"Oh." Raindrops clung to his dark hair. She watched, distracted, as a bead of water surrendered to gravity, dropped from his hair onto his cheek, then lazily rolled to the edge of his jaw. "You're soaked." To her chagrin, her voice sounded a little hoarse.

"Yeah. It's coming down pretty good."

"You'd better come in." Scooting back, she swiveled around, embarrassed by her reaction to him and praying he hadn't noticed. Yet despite her chagrin, she couldn't stop the tingle of awareness that tickled her spine as he followed her back down the hall and into her apartment. Heat painting her cheeks, she all but dashed to the bathroom.

She snatched a bath towel off the rack, fighting the urge to bury her head in it. *Really, Colleen! Grow up and quit acting like you're seventeen.*

It was excellent advice. Determined to follow it, she let out her breath, straightened her spine and turned.

And promptly bounced off Gavin's chest as she found him blocking the doorway.

"Oh! I didn't know you were there!" Despite her good intentions, she was helpless against the pleasure that zinged through her as he reached out to steady her.

Bravely, she ignored it, forcing herself to smile in the face of his dark, intent gaze. "I was thinking earlier how fortunate it was that the storm held off for the meeting. That everyone had time to get home before it really got ugly. But now here you are. All wet.'' Heaven help her, but she was babbling. The last time she could remember doing that was when Mother Superior had walked in on her doing her impression of the bishop, complete with an exaggerated Irish accent and his trademark steepled hands. Unnerved, she began to blot the moisture from the front of Gavin's jacket with the towel. ''You must be freezing—''

His hand came up, manacled her wrist. ''I'll do it,'' he said quietly.

She looked down at his long fingers. His skin was a shade darker than her own, his hands big but also elegant, his nails clean and clipped. For some reason, the sight of them made her even more acutely aware of the bathroom's diminutive size. And of how close they were standing.

And that she was anything but cold herself.

She released the towel as if it was on fire. ''Of course. I'll…'' Her voice failed for a moment. ''I'll just go make us some tea.'' Sliding her hand free of his grasp, she sidled past him with every intention of bolting for the relative safety of the kitchen.

"No."

The abruptness of his tone jerked her around. "I'm sorry?"

His dark eyes were impossible to read. "Don't go to any trouble for me. I don't plan to be here that long."

"Oh."

"I just want to talk to you for a second about Brett."

"Of course." She made a heroic effort to match his businesslike manner. "Why don't we go into the living room?" *Where you can warm up. And I can cool off. And where I'll be able to put some space between us until I can control my juvenile reaction to everything you say and do.*

"Great."

She crossed the hallway and entered the front room, where she headed for the small, upholstered, isolated armchair placed at right angles to the couch. Sitting, she curled her legs beneath her and tried to focus on the fire. Yet the room was so small she couldn't not see Gavin as he shrugged out of his jacket and tossed it over the umbrella stand inside the doorway. Or notice the way his well-defined biceps bulged and flexed beneath his thin black sweater as he rubbed his hair dry, finger-combed the silky strands into place, then tossed the towel on top of the jacket.

He took a look around. "This is…nice."

Something about the way he spoke suggested that he was surprised, which for some inexplicable reason helped restore a little of her usual equilibrium. "Thank you. How did it go with Brett?"

"Fine."

"Really?" *Way to go, Colleen. Could you sound any more surprised?*

But rather than take offense, Gavin gave a sigh, his mouth twisting in a self-deprecating smile. "Actually, that's a lie. Most of the night was pretty awful. I took him to the hotel, bought him dinner and did a first-rate job of making him feel out of place."

"Oh, dear."

"Yeah. But then later, on the drive back, I decided to give something else a try." He paced over to the windows, forcing her to twist around to keep him in sight. "I wanted him to realize that he and I do have some things in common... I showed him the place Lynette and I lived my last years of prep.''

For a moment she couldn't think what to say. While she'd known ever since being introduced to Gavin that he was from Jefferson Heights—he had, after all, been a scholarship student when Nick first brought him home and introduced him to the family—he'd always flatly refused to discuss specifics, much less show her or anyone else in her family where he actually lived.

So what? Surely you're not so petty you'd envy him and Brett the common bonds of youthful poverty and poor parenting?

Of course not.

''Did it help?'' she asked with genuine concern.

''Yeah. I think it did.'' He turned, walked over and sat down on the couch. ''At least he's willing to give things another chance. We're going to take in a Celtics game this weekend.''

''Gavin, that's wonderful!'' Impulsively she reached out and gave his forearm a squeeze.

The warm curve of muscle beneath her fingertips immediately went rigid, while his smile grew equally stiff. "I don't know about that, but it's an improvement over the mess I made of things earlier." He glanced at his wristwatch, then abruptly stood, sliding free of her touch in the process. "Hell, look at the time. It's after ten. I've intruded enough on your evening. I should get going."

What on earth was the matter with her? Every time he got the least bit close she either bolted or, worse, acted as if he were a sheet of paper and she a first-grader learning to finger-paint.

She scrambled to her feet. "I'm the one who ought to apologize," she said hastily, following in his wake like the tail on a kite as he strode over to get his jacket. "I should've told you more about Brett, made sure you understood how complicated he is. Not that he isn't terrific, with so much potential, but—"

"You don't have to sell him to me, Colleen." His voice unexpectedly curt, he stopped and turned. "If Brett wants me to, I'll be there for him. And when I make a commitment, I keep it."

She jerked to a halt, stopped as much by his slight emphasis on *I* as her desire not to crash into him. Not sure whether he was alluding to her decision to leave the Church or their breakup or both or neither one, she felt his words nevertheless cut straight to her heart. "Yes, of course. I didn't mean...I wasn't implying...that is, I wasn't trying to insult your integrity. I'm sorry."

Their gazes locked and the sudden silence in the room was deafening. As if from very faraway Colleen heard the fire snap, followed by the faint scrape of a tree branch against the window.

"Damn it, don't look like that," Gavin said fiercely.

She wasn't certain what it was he saw in her expression, but she was very certain she wanted to keep to herself the emotional turmoil he caused her. She lifted her chin. "I'm not. And don't curse."

"Don't you tell me what to do."

Having grown up with four brothers, she was fully versed in the folly of saying anything to the male of the species that resembled a challenge. Yet she couldn't stop the imprudent streak that seemed to seize control of her tongue. "Or what?"

His dark eyes hooded over. "Or this."

Clasping her upper arms, he lowered his head and in the next instant his mouth settled possessively over hers.

Four

——

The pleasure Colleen felt was immediate and stunning.

Pinpricks of delight raced down her spine at the hard warmth of Gavin's hands, the firm silkiness of his lips, the heat radiating off the solid angles of his muscular body.

For half a second she wondered what she was doing. Then she realized she didn't care. It had been so very, very long since she'd felt Gavin's touch. Oh, how she'd missed it. How she'd missed him.

She drank in his scent like a woman finding water after weeks in the desert. He smelled clean, like rain, shampoo and lemon drops, with a dash of something uniquely male that went straight to the core of her, making her feel weak in the knees.

But then, he'd always had that effect on her, from the very first time Nick had brought him home. Standing unobserved on the upper curve of the front stairway, she'd watched as her teenage brother's new friend had gotten his first glimpse of the sparkling floors and gleaming woodwork of her parents' entry.

As always, there'd been a tall vase of freshly cut flowers on the console table that faced the door. Though Nick had been too busy talking to notice it, she hadn't missed the way the newcomer had reached out and hesitantly touched the creamy petal of a deep-throated lily. There'd been a sort of wistful reverence to the gesture that had called out to her, touching a place in her heart.

As if he, too, had felt that tug of connection, Gavin had suddenly looked up. In the long moment they'd considered each other, Colleen had been overcome with an uncanny sense of familiarity, as if she'd always known him and understood his heart, his dreams, his strengths and vulnerabilities. Although she hadn't understood what was happening to her at the time, years later at college, when she and Gavin had finally acknowledged there was more between them than mere friendship and a mutual affection for Nick, she'd realized she'd fallen in love with him at that very first meeting.

Now it was years later—and nothing had changed.

Crowding closer, she raised her arms and tangled her fingers in his thick hair. Her pulse jumped as her thighs brushed his and her breasts met the hard wall of his chest.

She heard a soft little sound midway between a moan and a whimper, and vaguely recognized her own voice. Under different circumstances, with a different man, she would've been mortified. But this was Gavin. The only man she'd ever wanted. Without hesitation, she parted her lips for the probe of his tongue, savoring the bloom of heat that had her clenching her thighs as his tongue softly breached her mouth. With an instinct as old as time, she arched her back and crowded even closer, shivering with nervous wonder as the unmistakable thickness of his erection thrust against her.

Only to discover, too late, that apparently she'd made a mistake.

With a muffled curse, Gavin abruptly terminated their embrace and jerked away. "Damn it, Colleen! What do you think you're doing?"

She bit her throbbing lower lip, thinking the answer couldn't be any more obvious if she'd held up a flashing neon sign that read "Wildly enjoying kissing you and thinking I wouldn't mind doing more."

And yet it was clear from the look on Gavin's face that would definitely *not* be an acceptable thing to say. Struggling valiantly to rein in her jangling senses, she tried to decide what would be a more diplomatic but still-honest answer. "I...your kiss...it caught me by surprise. I didn't think that you...that is, I didn't expect that I...and then, it just felt so—"

He threw up a hand like a cop halting traffic, putting what Colleen could only view as a humane stop to the fit and start of her words. Her relief vanished, however, when he said, "This is all my fault. I was out of line to take advantage of your innocence that way. Way out of line."

"Oh, but—"

"I shouldn't have come here. I knew that, but I came, anyway. Now the best thing I can do is leave." Shoving a hand through his already tousled hair, he twisted around and snatched up his jacket.

"But, Gavin—"

"I'm sorry, Colleen."

Without giving her a chance to say more, he strode to her front door, and had it open and was passing through it by the time her addled brain accepted that he really meant to go. "Gavin, wait!" She scrambled after him. Dashing out of the apartment, she raced down the hall and finally caught up with him in the entryway. "Please." Although logically she knew she was incapable of physically restraining him, she reached out and grabbed hold of his shoulder, anyway.

A shudder went through him at her touch and he spun around. *"Don't."*

She snatched back her hand, startled by his vehemence. "I'm sorry."

"Aw, sh—" He clenched his teeth as he bit off the curse. "Do *not* apologize, Colleen. You've got nothing to be sorry about. Like I said before, I'm the one at fault here."

She opened her mouth to protest, then shut it as it occurred to her that if she ever wanted to see him again, and she did, this might not be the best time to tell him he had no reason to apologize, either. That she'd wanted to kiss him ever since the wedding reception, and that far from being a hapless victim he'd overpowered with his virile magnetism, she'd more than welcomed his embrace.

She dampened her lips; the Almighty was no doubt going to get her for what she was about to do. "If you're truly sincere about believing you were out of line, there's a way you can make it up to me."

Gavin suddenly looked just the slightest bit wary. "Yeah? And what's that?"

"My family's having a little get-together to launch the newest Baronessa gelato flavor. Come with me."

Gavin stared at her as if she'd lost her mind. "You're kidding, right?"

"No."

"Under the circumstances, I don't think that's a very good idea."

"On the contrary. It will be nice and public and will give us a chance to talk in depth about Brett and the challenges he's facing. It's not as if it would be a…a date, or anything." Poor Father Brennan. He was going to get an awful shock when he heard her confession on Sunday.

Gavin considered her for a moment so long it felt like an eternity, then heaved a sigh. "When is it?"

"Friday." Her hopes skyrocketed, only to plummet as he yanked open the door.

"I'll think about it, okay?"

"But how will I know—"

"I'll call you." And with that the door banged shut and he was gone.

Frustrated in more ways than one, Colleen let loose a sigh of her own. Terrific. Now, in addition to everything else, every time the phone rang for the next few days she was going to have to deal with a case of yo-yo stomach.

Apparently the Lord wasn't wasting any time getting her started on her penance.

Some little get-together.

Taking a sip of champagne, Gavin lowered his wineglass and considered the scores of people crowding the reception area of Baronessa's main corporate headquarters.

In addition to most of the Barone family and dozens of their longtime friends and key employees, a number of local restaurateurs and dignitaries were in attendance, including several national food writers. And because today just happened to be Valentine's Day, a little fact Colleen hadn't seen fit to mention when she'd asked him to come and he'd completely overlooked when he'd agreed to attend, a sizable number of the Boston press was covering the event, no doubt considering it good local color.

God knew, the family had spared no expense. Dozens and dozens of huge bouquets of red roses in genuine cut-crystal vases decorated the room, giving it an air of festive elegance. Add the quintet of ornate fountains spouting champagne and the constantly circulating tuxedo-clad catering staff, and he had to give the Barones credit. They knew how to throw a party.

Under different circumstances Gavin might even have enjoyed himself. Say, for example, if he'd been here because the family was courting his business.

But that wasn't the case. Hell, no. No matter what kind of twist he tried to put on it, he was here tonight because of Colleen.

He considered her as she stood a few feet away, listening intently to her younger sister Rita, who was talking and gesturing animatedly.

At first glance, Colleen, the oldest of the Barone daughters, looked perfectly respectable. Her makeup was a study in elegant understatement, just a kiss of color at her eyes, cheeks and lips. And the gleaming, slightly tousled cap of her hair was exceedingly casual compared to some of the other women's more ornate upsweeps or geled, cutting-edge hairdos. Likewise, her wine-colored dress with its high neck and long sleeves was outwardly demure and almost plain.

Until you noticed that it was made of some sort of stretchy lace material that clung to her every slender curve. And that it exposed tantalizing glimpses of smooth, peachy skin every time she moved. Which was about the same time you began to wonder how much of the plum color glistening on the full curve of her lips was lipstick and how much was just her. And then, try as you might, you couldn't help but remember how silky her unlaquered hair felt against your fingertips, and how...

Whispering a curse, Gavin tossed back the last of his bubbly. There was a stir at the far end of the room, and grateful for the diversion, he dragged his gaze away from the pale, vulnerable curve of Colleen's neck and along with everyone else, turned to watch as her father, Carlo, took center stage on a low dais. Facing the crowd, the older man waited for silence before he spoke.

''Welcome, friends,'' he said, smiling genially. ''On behalf of my family and everyone who works at Baronessa, I thank you for coming tonight.''

Gavin felt a tingle run down his spine and knew, without turning his head, that Colleen had come to stand at his side.

"We at Baronessa pride ourselves on making only the finest gelato from the highest-quality ingredients from around the world," Carlo continued. "To that end we are always extremely selective before we introduce a new flavor, testing and tasting and tinkering with the recipe until we are one hundred percent certain it will live up to the Baronessa reputation for excellence.

"And as I'm sure you all know—" Carlo leaned forward, as if imparting a great secret to his closest friends "—that means that only a very few, very unique, very special new flavors get the privilege of becoming part of our line.

"And that is why we are so very proud to introduce to you tonight the newest jewel in the Baronessa crown." With a crook of his fingers he beckoned to the left, and a procession of waiters holding high over their heads silver trays loaded with scoops of deep raspberry-colored dessert nestled in sparkling glasses began to enter the room. "We've named it passionfruit.'' He gave a dramatic flourish, a sudden twinkle lighting his eyes. ''And when better than St. Valentine's Day to unveil it, eh?''

There was a burst of appreciative laughter. It was quickly followed by a spontaneous swell of applause as the Barone patriarch gave a genial nod and exhorted everyone to enjoy the new icy treat as the waiters began to move through the crowd distributing it.

Gavin turned to Colleen. ''That was a pretty good show. I can see your father hasn't lost either his flair or his enthusiasm for the business.''

''Yes and no.'' She glanced at the older man, and Gavin didn't miss the way her face softened as she watched him accept a bowl of his company's newest creation. ''Papa loves everything about it and always will, from actually making the gelato to marketing it to scooping cones at the gelateria on Hanover Street. But when it comes to the nuts and bolts of the day-to-day operation, Nick, Joe and Gina have taken over more and more of it the past few years.''

Gavin gave a slight shrug. ''I guess it's

bound to happen as his generation ages and ours grows up." He paused. "I heard about Joseph losing his wife. That must've been tough."

She nodded, her expression sobering as she considered her always serious second-eldest brother. "It was, but he's doing all right. Although now that Nick and Gail are settled, I suppose he'll be Mother's next matrimonial target." Her lips quirked mischievously. "That is, if she doesn't find out about Rita first."

He raised an eyebrow in question. "Rita?"

"Uh-huh. It seems someone sent my little sister an anonymous gift today, of all things. She appears to have acquired a secret admirer and is going crazy trying to figure out who it is. But not nearly as crazy as she'll be if Mother finds out about it and decides to 'help' her discover her mystery man's identity."

"It doesn't sound like your mom's changed much." Gavin did his best to make his voice light, but it wasn't easy. Moira Barone had been coolly polite but nothing more when he and Nick had become friends, and as a teenager, each time he'd visited the Barone brownstone he'd always suspected that the second he left she'd made a beeline to the silver to count it.

And though later on, her opinion of him had never become an issue since he and Colleen had broken up before they'd gotten around to informing her family they were a couple, he was pretty damn certain Mrs. Barone would not have considered him a suitable suitor for her daughter.

As if reading his mind, a shadow passed briefly over Colleen's face, only to vanish as she determinedly summoned a smile. "No, I'm afraid you're right. One can always count on Mama to be Mama—just like death or taxes. Although—" her smile grew more genuine "—if you ever quote me as saying that, I'll deny it to my very last breath."

To his surprise, Gavin found he couldn't help but smile back, which sent a jolt of uneasiness through him. He was also surprised by the accompanying thought that Colleen was no longer the young woman he'd known more than a decade ago. She'd changed.

Well, yeah, Einstein, what did you expect?

Up until not too long ago, she was a nun.
That's bound to change anyone.

"Oh, dear."

The totally unexpected note of alarm in Colleen's voice jarred him out of his reverie. Pushing his unsettled thoughts to the back burner, he shifted his focus and took a good look at her, concerned as he saw that her eyes were wide with growing alarm as she glanced around at the surrounding crowd. "What's the matter?"

"I don't know. But there seems to be something wrong. Look at Mr. Marino." She indicated a short, paunchy gentleman who looked to be about her father's age.

Sure enough, the older man appeared to be in distress. His face was red, his eyes watering, his breath coming in raspy gasps as he stared accusingly at the ice-cream bowl still clutched in one hand. Tossing his spoon away with a clatter, he reached over, snatched a champagne glass off the nearest table and took a hearty gulp, only to promptly begin to sputter even harder.

Nor was he alone, Gavin realized as he took a quick survey of the crowd. Dozens of people toward the front of the room—those who'd been first to be served Baronessa's new dessert—were showing various signs of distress, albeit less severe than Mr. Marino's, from scrubbing at their mouths, to indelicately spitting spoonfuls of gelato back into their bowls, to coughing as they struggled to get air, to fanning their faces and dashing tears from their eyes.

"Call 911," Gavin said to Colleen. "There's something in the ice cream that shouldn't be there."

"Oh, but that can't be—"

"Make the call," he ordered crisply, "and we'll argue about it later." He waited a second for her to head off to find a phone, then crossed to Mr. Marino and slipped the bowl out of the older man's unresisting hand. Dipping a finger into the gelato, he touched it lightly to his lips.

In less time than it took to light a match, the affected part of his mouth felt as if it had encountered a blowtorch.

"What the hell is going on?"

The alarmed sound of his old friend Nick's voice turned him around, and he found the other man standing no more than a few feet away, his legs splayed in a fighter's aggressive stance and a combination of concern, frustration and anger darkening his good-looking face.

''I think something caustic's been added to your gelato,'' Gavin said, keeping his voice down since he didn't want to alarm the people around them. ''Maybe some sort of pepper, judging by the way my lip feels right now, numb and tingling at the same time. For almost everyone, it doesn't seem to be causing anything more than discomfort.'' He glanced over at Mr. Marino, who seemed to be having some trouble breathing. ''But that gentleman seems to be getting worse.''

''Did anyone call 911?'' Nick couldn't hide the alarm in his voice.

''Yes, Colleen did. The paramedics should be on their way.'' Gavin clapped his hand on his friend's shoulder. ''In the meantime you might want to make some sort of announcement telling everyone to lay off the champagne. If it is a pepper or some sort of derivative, booze will just make the burning worse.

A piece of bread or a cracker would be better."

"What does this look like, the Fourth Street Deli?" Nick demanded. Despite his tension, he reached out and shook Gavin's hand. "Thanks. I promise I'll buy you a drink when this is all over and you can tell me how you got so smart."

"You've got yourself a deal." Glad to have been able to help, if only a little, Gavin watched Nick stride away, purpose and determination in his every step as he began rattling out orders to a variety of people, including several of his brothers and sisters.

Stripping off his jacket and tossing it over a chair in anticipation of following Nick's lead, Gavin realized how much he'd missed his friend these past few years, missed his energy and intelligence and his basic goodness.

But not nearly as much as he'd missed Nick's little sister, he belatedly realized as he turned to find Colleen standing only an arm's length away, watching him with unmistakable admiration in her eyes.

Twelve years ago, he would've done just

about anything to see her look at him that way.

He made a sudden vow that for tonight, at least, he wasn't going to let her get away.

Five

There was nothing quite so pathetic as a thirty-two-year-old virgin plotting seduction, Colleen reflected as she stood in her kitchen hours later, waiting impatiently for the teapot to whistle. Every neuron in her body tingled and twitched at the thought of Gavin O'Sullivan waiting for her in her living room. Just as they had throughout the evening, especially when she watched him commandingly take charge of the scene at Baronessa headquarters. During that whole time she couldn't stop thinking of what she'd like to do when they were alone later.

She wished she could believe that after the debacle of the gelato-tasting earlier tonight, the evening could only improve. Yet she had a strong suspicion that when it came to matters of the flesh or, she supposed, most anything else, it didn't quite work that way.

If only she had more experience. Heavens, if only she had *any* experience. She was a relatively intelligent woman; why had it never occurred to her after she'd left the order to find someone on whom she could practice her feminine wiles?

Well, let's see... Could it be because no one except Gavin has ever interested you that way?

She suppressed the urge to roll her eyes, but just barely. After all, it was her tendency to follow her heart, instead of using her head that had resulted in her present predicament.

Not that bemoaning her past—or, more precisely, her lack of one—was going to improve matters. Yet even so, she couldn't seem to stop wishing there was some way to make certain that if she made the first move tonight, it wouldn't end up like her and Gavin's last encounter, with him bolting for the door.

Unfortunately if there was one thing she'd learned over the past dozen years, it was that absolutely nothing, with the obvious exception of God's love, came with guarantees.

Good grief, Colleen, with just a smidgen more effort you're going to talk yourself out of a moderate case of nerves and into a full-blown panic attack. And won't Gavin find that alluring?

She had a vision of herself running into the living room babbling that confession was good for the soul and demanding to know if Gavin found her the least bit attractive, because she really, really, really wanted to kiss him silly and more. So much more.

She gave a violent start as she heard a floorboard creak. Freezing in place, she held her breath, then realized it was only Gavin moving around in her living room. With a slight shake of her head, she exhaled and raised her hands to the fiery heat throbbing in her cheeks.

The mere idea of putting herself in such an emotionally charged situation might have been laughable if she'd been in the mood to see the slightest humor. But she wasn't exactly the dancing-on-the-edge type, and with each passing moment she became less and less certain what Gavin's reaction would be if she actually had the courage to follow through on her desires.

It was not a comforting thought. Even so, a persistent thread of sensual excitement kept drawing her mind back to the enticing image of his mouth. And to the way his every movement hinted at the hard muscle beneath his smooth, olive-toned skin and how the most innocent touch of his long-fingered hands made her nerves sing with pleasure—

The shrill of a ringing phone snapped her out of her growing fantasy that, with any luck, she was going to finally make love to Gavin tonight.

Oh, sure, she thought as she reached for her cordless phone. And right after that she was going to sprout wings and fly. "Hello?"

"Hey, Col, it's Nick."

Relief flooded through her at the sound of her brother's voice. "Thank goodness. I've been hoping you'd call. Is everyone okay? How's Mr. Marino?" The last she'd seen of the neighborhood friend of her sister Gina he was being taken away in an ambulance. "And is Papa all right?"

"Papa's fine—if you don't count his being mad as hell about what happened. Everyone's okay, but the doctor wants to keep an eye on Mr. Marino. Apparently he was allergic to whatever was put into the gelato and he had some trouble breathing. They call it anaphylaxis."

"I still can't believe it really happened," Colleen said. "Thank heaven he is going to be all right. That could have been tragic."

"Don't think I haven't thought of that," Nick said grimly. "We were just lucky Gavin happened to be there and could give us a head start on what to do."

"Yes." Even though she knew it was silly, she felt a sort of possessive pride every time she thought about how calm, controlled and effective Gavin had been in the face of the crisis. "We were."

"Yeah, well, be sure and tell him thanks."

She wasn't quite sure how to respond to Nick's certainty that Gavin was there with her.

Thankfully she was saved by the shrill whistle of the tea kettle. "Nick, I've got to go."

"Okay. But do me a favor and tell Gavin I'll call him tomorrow."

"Sure." Disconnecting, she set the phone on the counter and turned off the burner, then reached for the French coffee press, which she'd already filled with freshly ground coffee beans. While the coffee steeped, she got down two cups, some napkins and a tin of cookies and assembled a tray. Then, telling herself firmly that she wasn't going to let her brother's unintended interference put a wrench in her plans, she picked up the tray, took a deep breath and headed for the living room.

Seconds later she concluded that breathing was highly overrated. And that while just a little while ago she might have truly believed she was much too conservative and inexperienced, not to mention repressed, to actually follow through on her kitchen fantasies, that was no longer true.

All it took was one look at Gavin. Because while she'd been working herself into a lather in the other room, he'd shed his coat, loosened his tie and undone the top few buttons of his shirt.

Now, sprawled comfortably on the center of the couch, his legs stretched out and his hands clasped loosely behind his head, he was the picture of potent masculinity. And, she acknowledged, her dream lover come true.

"Gavin?" Her voice sounded every bit as tremulous as she felt.

"Yeah?"

"Nick called. He said to say thanks and wanted me to let you know that it looks as if everyone's going to be fine."

"Good."

She swallowed, her mouth suddenly feeling desert-dry. "I—I have a question."

"Okay. Shoot."

"Do you really want to have a cup of coffee?"

He glanced from her face to the tray in her hands and back again. "Hey, listen, if there's some problem, if you're worried you made it too weak or too strong, it's no big deal—"

"That's not it."

"Oh." He considered her, clearly puzzled. "Okay."

She felt his gaze like a brand as she walked the few feet to the sideboard, set down the tray, then turned and, heart jammed in her throat, approached the couch.

He studied her face, then cocked his head slightly to one side. "So, you want to tell me what's going on?"

"Want to?" She grimaced. "Not really. But I will." And before she could lose her nerve, she closed the distance between them. "The truth is, I don't want anything to drink. And I don't want to sit here and make polite conversation.

"What I want—" She stopped to clear her throat. "The only thing I want is you." In one decisive motion she swung a leg over his thighs, straddling them, slid her arms around his neck and her bottom onto his lap, and claimed his mouth with her own.

She braced for his reaction, her heart in her throat.

She didn't have long to wait. For the space of a heartbeat every muscle in his body tightened, and then to her profound relief he made a raw, primitive sound low in his throat, wrapped his arms around her and met her kiss with his own.

Time lost all meaning for Colleen. She wasn't sure how long they kissed, whether it was seconds or minutes or hours. Nor did she care. The only thing in the whole wide world that mattered was Gavin; his taste, his touch, the wet heat of his mouth.

When finally they came up for air, she felt as if every nerve ending in her body was on fire. She blinked, knowing there was something she needed to tell him and wondering what on earth had happened to her verbal skills. Her mind was a blank. "That was nice," she ventured.

Gavin clearly wasn't in the mood for conversation. "Oh, yeah," he murmured. In the next instant he nuzzled her neck with his lips, honing in on the hollow behind her ear.

The warm lick of his tongue followed by the cooler tickle of his breath sent a shock of pure pleasure shooting through her. Feeling blissfully weak, she let her head loll back, allowing him greater access even as she again tried to remember what she'd wanted to say.

A wisp of recollection drifted across her

mind. "There's—" she gasped as his teeth closed with gentle firmness on her earlobe "—something I need to tell you."

"Yeah?"

He nibbled at the lower curve of her ear. To her stupefaction, that relatively tame action made her nipples instantly begin to throb, while a feeling of warmth and wetness blossomed at the apex of her thighs. It was so unexpected that her mind blanked out again, and it was a minute or two before she could speak.

Not that what she wanted to say seemed as urgent now as it had just a few minutes ago. Still… "I'm wearing panty hose."

"What?"

"You know, panty hose? The kind that comes in the little plastic packages at the grocery store. I'm so sorry, but…I thought you should know."

He was silent just long enough for her to start to wonder if she'd been right to tell him when he abruptly leaned back to stare at her. "Why on earth would you think you had to tell me that?" he demanded.

He sounded so incredulous that for the first time she felt a little foolish. "Well, you've dated all those glamorous models and gorgeous actresses and I'm sure they all have silk panties and gorgeous underwear and garters and lace, but I—I don't.''

Without warning, he gave a muffled bark of laughter. ''Oh, yeah, that's a real cold shower, all right.'' He stroked a rough-tipped thumb down the curve of her cheek. ''Baby, you could be dressed in sackcloth and ashes—or better yet, nothing at all—and I'd still think you were the sexiest woman on earth. You seem to have forgotten that I've wanted you since I was seventeen years old.''

''Oh, Gavin. Really?''

''Sure.''

''But you never said…''

He gave a slight, dismissive shrug. ''How could you not have known? I was crazy about you. And unlike you women, that's a pretty hard fact for us guys to hide.''

As if to prove his point, he rolled her beneath him and settled himself in the cradle of her thighs. Even through the barrier of their clothes, there was no missing the rock-solid length of his erection pressing against her. ''I want you. Colleen, I want you so much.''

"Me, too," she replied, finding it hard to talk due to the combination of relief and anticipation surging through her. Locking her hands around his neck, she urged him closer.

Yet to her surprise he momentarily resisted. Instead, he lifted himself up on one elbow, slid his hand down her thigh until he found the hem of her dress, then slipped his fingers beneath it. Ignoring her indrawn breath, he slowly ran his warm palm up the inside of her thigh.

"As for these—" there was no mistaking the flame of satisfaction that lit his eyes as he reached the crotch of her silky hose and his hands brushed tantalizing against her "—no problem. No problem at all." With clever fingers he lightly began to stroke her, intuitively seeming to know just the motion and the pressure to please her.

One did not shake off thirty-two years of good-girl behavior, however, without making one token, knee-jerk act of resistance. Which was why she found herself automatically lifting her hand with some sort of hazy, totally lacking-in-conviction idea that he really shouldn't be doing *that*.

Then he gently pressed down and rotated his thumb dead center against the one place on her entire body screaming loudest to be touched.

It was as if the rest of her ceased to exist. Her hand fell bonelessly back to the couch as every nerve in her body made a mass migration to the tingling, tightening, escalating swell of sensation beneath Gavin's fingertips.

She couldn't move, couldn't think, couldn't utter even the tiniest sound as her entire being strained toward an elusive need that stubbornly seemed to lurk just a fraction beyond her reach.

And then Gavin slid a little lower on the couch, shifted his head and clamped his mouth around one of her nipples straining through the lace dress and sucked at the same instant he rotated his thumb against her again—and pushed her over the edge.

Pleasure unlike anything she'd ever felt rocketed through her. It claimed every muscle and every nerve ending, every inch of bone and patch of skin. And it seemed to go on forever.

And ever.

And ever.

By the time the tempest finally passed thousands of seconds later, she felt amazed, transformed, exhausted, exalted and reborn.

And happier than she'd been in a long, long time.

It was a Sally Field moment if there'd ever been one, she decided as she found herself thinking, *He likes me. He really likes me.*

It seemed like something she really ought to share. Not the Sally Field part, of course, although she couldn't stop the smile tugging at her lips as a little voice in her head insisted that he had to care about her to have done something so intimate. But surely he had every right to know that she thought the entire thing had been amazing. That *he'd* been amazing.

"Gavin?" Opening her eyes, she looked down, her stomach hollowing with a combination of tenderness and awe at the sight of his head cradled against her breast.

"What?"

"That was…incredible."

"I'm glad you think so." He lifted his head and twisted his neck to meet her gaze, and her heart did a wild little somersault.

Because in stark contrast to the languid satisfaction she hadn't a doubt was plastered all over her face, the line of his mouth was taut and the slash of his cheekbones pronounced, while his dark eyes glittered with raw desire.

A little drumbeat of anticipation kicked up inside her, miraculously banishing her previous lethargy. "And why is that?" she inquired in a throaty voice that didn't sound at all like hers.

"Because." In one lithe move his feet hit the floor at that same time that he scooped her up and into his arms. "That was just the beginning."

"It was?"

"Oh, yeah. There's not a whole lot you can count on in life—" he straightened, lifting her as if she weighed nothing and began to walk, carrying her out of the living room and down the short hall in the direction of her bedroom "—but you can stake your life on that."

So far, so good, Gavin thought as he bumped open Colleen's bedroom door with his hip.

Somehow he was managing to control himself, to walk and talk and act like a civilized grown-up despite the near-savage need pumping through his veins and making his heart pound like a jackhammer.

He shifted sideways as he crossed the threshold to ensure he didn't inadvertently scrape Colleen against the frame, filled with the old protective instinct she'd always inspired in him. The one that until half an hour ago he'd been one hundred percent certain was not merely dead but buried six feet deep. The one that now appeared to have magically resurrected itself.

And wasn't that just perfect? Because at the same time, he was caught in a vise of desire stronger than any he'd ever experienced. So compelled was he to touch, taste and bury himself inside this one particular woman that the mere thought of being thwarted made him feel frantic and desperate and more than a little dangerous.

And he didn't like it. He didn't like it one bit. Because although he could no longer recall the specifics that had prompted it—only that it had predictably involved his mother abandoning him yet again to pursue her own selfish pleasures—he'd long ago vowed never to care too much about anything or anyone.

Yet here he was, frantic with need. Hell, he was so turned on by the mere act of holding Colleen in his arms that his body, like that of some randy, inexperienced teenager, was on the verge of embarrassing him. And all because of a woman who'd already stomped his heart into the ground once, more than proving she couldn't be trusted.

And yet as he looked down into her soft blue eyes, he knew that he would never allow anything to hurt her.

The realization sent a deep wave of uneasiness surging through him.

"Gavin?"

Just the sound of his name on her lips was as tantalizing as any caress. His body jerked in eager response, and the effort it took to control it put an abrupt end to his disturbing thoughts.

"Are you all right?" she asked.

"Sure. Why wouldn't I be?"

"I don't know." She pursed her lips in contemplation and it took all of his willpower not to just toss her down on the bed, rip away the bare minimum of clothes that would give him access to what he wanted most and plunge himself deep inside her. "You just seem a little…tense."

No kidding. His entire body from his hair to his toes hurt from the effort of keeping himself in check, and there was a fine trickle of perspiration trailing down his back, further proof of the escalating cost of his restraint. "Yeah. I suppose I do. I've waited a long time for this. For you."

Her eyes momentarily widened and then she reached out to cup the side of his face in one fine-boned hand. "Me, too," she said softly.

He appreciated the sentiment. Still, the more cynical side of him, the part she'd had no small part in helping to create, seriously doubted she truly understood what she'd put him through all those years ago.

The whole time they'd been together he'd had to constantly rein himself in, denying the howling needs of his testosterone-flooded body. Yet he'd assured himself over and over that it was worth it, persuaded that what they had would last forever and that he could wait—he *would* wait—to make her his wife before claiming her innocence.

It had been his willing gift to her, one of the few he could give her and a testament to his belief that she was the antithesis of the women around whom he'd grown up. He'd believed with all his heart that she was pure, gentle, *good.*

Right up until the minute she'd told him that it was over. That they both needed to concentrate on school. That, when it came right down to it, they weren't right for each other.

But that was then and this was now, he reminded himself. He was no longer a welfare kid from the projects, going to school on a soccer scholarship, working multiple jobs to make ends meet.

Just as Colleen was no longer a sheltered young innocent, as she'd so amply demonstrated in the living room just minutes ago.

And although sometime in the past few days the last lingering little sting of being dumped by her had vanished, he wasn't so foolish as to believe that by being together now they could turn back the clock or recapture what they'd lost.

But there was no reason they shouldn't enjoy tonight. He knew he intended to. And as his body wasn't the least bit shy about reminding him, it was past time they got started.

Reaching the end of the bed, he set Colleen on her feet and unclasped her hands from around his neck. Then in one fluid motion he reached down, grasped the bottom edge of her stretchy little dress, pulled it up and over her head and tossed it aside.

She made a little sound that was part gasp, part protest and part laugh. "Gavin—"

"No." He pressed a finger to her lips. "Don't say a thing. Just…let me do this."

Her blue eyes searched his, and whatever she saw there caused her expression to abruptly sober. She swallowed, then, her gaze still locked on his face, nodded.

He reached around, unsnapped her bra and slid it away, then hooked his thumbs in the waistband of her panty hose, slid them down and snagged the side of her panties and peeled both garments to her ankles. He gave her just enough time to grip his shoulders for balance and then sent her shoes sailing away. The remainder of her undergarments followed seconds later.

He straightened, took a step back and looked.

Instantly he was grateful that he regularly worked out. Otherwise he probably would've dropped dead from a heart attack.

She was perfect. Petite, but willowy. Sleek, silky-skinned, delicately boned. She was more beautiful than he'd ever imagined, and over the course of seventeen years, he'd imagined, a lot.

Her breasts were small, but exquisitely shaped, tipped with pale pink nipples that were currently beaded like priceless pearls. Beneath the smooth plane of her stomach, the perfect dimple of her navel, a neat triangle of ebony curls seemed to point the way to his ultimate destination.

The second he could breathe again, he yanked his shirt over his head, heedless of the sound of popping buttons, stripped away his pants, briefs and socks and eliminated the distance between them.

Then he caught her to him with an arm to her waist and one to the top of her thighs and lifted her up. Their lips met and clung. Having felt her silky wetness through her clothing out in the living room, he didn't hesitate. Knowing she was more than ready, he bent his knees and with one powerful thrust sheathed himself inside her.

"Oh! Gavin, oh!"

Her exclamation of shocked pleasure was the most potent of aphrodisiacs. Not that he needed any added stimulation. Lowering her onto the bed, settling deeper into the notch of her thighs, he had to fight a primitive urge to say to hell with control and just do whatever it took to accomplish his own pleasure.

Except that he wanted…more. He wanted Colleen twisting and bucking beneath him, he wanted her shuddering and shaking, he wanted her shouting his name as she came.

Bracing on his forearms, he came up on his knees, searching for just the perfect angle. Knowing he'd found it when she gave a surprised little shudder, he tore his mouth from her lips and traced a line with his tongue from her throat to the shallow valley between her breasts.

"I…that's… I didn't realize…" Her breathless attempts to talk ceased abruptly as he licked one tightly budded nipple, gently blew on it, then locked onto it with his mouth and sucked. Hard.

With a strangled cry she lifted her hips and took him as deeply as she could, then did an instinctive bump and grind that was as old as time.

It did him in.

With a deep, guttural sound of his own, he lifted himself up and began to move, out and then back in, harder and faster, faster and harder. The small of his back hollowed, the bands of muscle that sheathed his solar plexus clenched, his biceps burned.

A rictus of pure, possessive satisfaction tugged the corners of his mouth as he heard her breathy moans and felt her strong interior muscles clench and release around him.

This is the best sex I've ever had in my life. Nothing's ever felt this good, this right.

It was as if he and Colleen were the perfect fit, absolutely made for each other.

It was his last rational thought before his climax hit him with the force of a runaway train, carrying him into a void of pure, mind-numbing pleasure.

Six

"So there you are."

Seated at the end of the richly patterned brocade sofa that graced her father's cozy study, Colleen looked up from the magazine she'd been reading as her younger sister Gina swept into the room.

In a ritual instituted by their mother, Moira, when Colleen, Nick, Ryan and Joe, the four older kids, had been teenagers, barring death or imprisonment the entire family was expected to sit down to dinner together at their parents' Beacon Hill home the second Sunday of each month—or face their mother's wrath.

Not surprisingly, attendance was excellent. And usually Colleen genuinely enjoyed the chance to visit with her brothers and sisters and get brought up to date on their lives.

But not tonight. Tonight she couldn't stop thinking about how Gavin was at her place helping Brett with a homework assignment. And how she could hardly wait for the clock to strike seven-thirty, the earliest acceptable time for post-dinner departure. Or that as usual, God seemed to be having some fun at her expense, since the time, which usually flew by at these little get-togethers, currently seemed to be hobbling along with all the speed of a three-legged tortoise climbing Mount Everest.

"I wondered where you were hiding." With her usual efficiency, Gina made a quick survey of the room, then headed to the fireplace, where she stooped down in order to open the screen. Taking a stick of applewood from the bin on the hearth, she tossed it onto the dwindling flames before straightening and turning to address Colleen. "What happened? All the arguing and shouting finally get to be too much for you?''

Colleen shook her head and a little regretfully slid the magazine—a copy of *American Bride* that she assumed had originally belonged to Nick's new wife, Gail—onto the end table. "Of course not. Besides, you know what Mother always says, 'Barones do not shout. They discuss.'" She tipped up her chin in a lofty way that was a dead-on imitation of their maternal parent "'Albeit with passionate persistence.'"

Clearly caught off guard, Gina let out a surprised sputter of laughter, and some of the tension seemed to drain out of her. Plopping down on the sofa next to Colleen, she kicked off her shoes and stretched out her long, slender legs. "Thanks. I needed that. I'm pretty sure it's the first time I've laughed in the past forty-eight hours." Unable to contain a slight shudder, she leaned her head back against the cushion, squeezed her eyes shut and let out a heartfelt sigh. "Lord, what a nightmare."

There was no need for her to explain that she was referring to the Valentine's Day disaster; Friday night's debacle had been the dominant topic most of the night. And since Gina was Baronessa's VP in charge of marketing and public relations, it had fallen on her slim shoulders to deal with the press the past forty-eight hours and do what she could to minimize the damage done to the company's reputation. She'd been in the thick of every discussion.

Colleen leaned over and gave her sister a quick hug. Pulling back, she met Gina's troubled gaze. "It'll be all right," she said softly. "Just give it some time. You're doing a great job."

"I don't know about that," Gina said with a sigh. "Every time I think about all those people getting sick because some twisted creep put habanera peppers into the gelato, I want to hit someone. And who ever even *heard* of a burning-hot pepper that's colorless and odorless and flavorless, anyway?" Her slim, elegant hands curled into fists. "It was probably one of those sneaky, underhanded, weasel-faced Contis."

Colleen checked her instinctive protest. Although there was no proof that the feud with their family's long-term archenemies was behind what had happened Friday night, feelings for and against the theory were running high.

While Nick, as chief operating officer, insisted it was his obligation to remain neutral until he had all the facts, their father, Carlo, cousins Daniel and Derrick, and Gina herself obviously were convinced what had happened had to be the work of the Contis.

Their brother Joe and cousin Claudia, on the other hand, were more inclined to believe that one of Baronessa's competitors must have been behind the malicious act.

Most unexpected of all, however, had been Maria. Almost ten years younger than Colleen and the baby of the family at twenty-three, the very capable manager of the Hanover Street gelateria had out of the blue unexpectedly defended the Contis, causing a mild uproar and a lot of raised eyebrows.

Colleen wasn't sure what she believed. Like Nick, it wasn't in her nature to rush to judgment. And she had faith that a certain Higher Power would see to it that things eventually got sorted out and justice prevailed.

Plus, at the moment she happened to be

more than a little preoccupied with her own life.

As if reading her mind, Gina suddenly turned to her. "You certainly didn't have much to say at dinner one way or the other."

Colleen met her sister's lovely violet eyes and shrugged. "I guess I don't see the need. I'm confident that you and Papa and Nick and Joe will get to the bottom of it."

Gina shook her head in a show of disbelief. "You know, sometimes I can't believe we're related. You're always so sensible and serene."

Don't I wish, Colleen thought wryly. Serene was the very last word she'd use to describe herself ever since the incredible night she'd spent with Gavin. Instead, she felt like one of those tiny figures inside a well-shaken snow globe—totally adrift and completely clueless as to which way was up and which was down.

"Although," Gina mused out loud, tilting her head a fraction as she considered her sister, "tonight you do seem a little distracted. And once or twice you've had the strangest little smile on your face." He gaze abruptly sharpened. "It doesn't have something to do with your seeing Gavin O'Sullivan again, does it?"

The small brass clock on the mantel chimed. Colleen glanced at her watch, saw that it was finally half-past seven and scrambled to her feet.

"You're imagining things," she said, trying not to wince as she added *lying* to her growing list of recent sins. She slipped on her shoes, leaned over and gave a startled Gina a quick hug. "But I love you, anyway," she said. "And don't worry so much. Everything will turn out all right."

"But, Colleen, wait! Where are you going?"

She flashed her sister a sunny smile. "Home."

The last place Colleen expected to find Gavin and Brett was out behind the brownstone in the garage with Mr. Crypinski.

In the three years she'd lived there, she'd never been allowed into the small, detached building with its boarded windows. Her landlord had always kept it securely locked.

Colleen had to admit that Mr. Crypinski's

protective, secretive behavior had caused her no end of entertaining speculation. What could he have in there? she'd often wondered. An alien spacecraft? The world's largest collection of old magazines? A gigantic ball of string? Or perhaps there was a cache of super high-tech spy equipment because behind his gruff, taciturn facade the older man was actually a suave secret agent, South Boston's very own James Bond. Although even she realized that last was a definite long shot.

But now, as she stood in the garage's open doorway looking in at the scene, which was as bright as day thanks to a bank of lights overhead, Colleen finally knew.

And it was even better and more unexpected than anything she'd ever imagined.

Smack dab in the center of the concrete slab floor was a car. And not just any car. Having been blessed with four brothers, Colleen knew a classic 1961 Thunderbird when she saw one.

And this one was a beaut. Looking as if it had just rolled off the line and onto the showroom floor, the candy-apple-red convertible boasted a mirror-polished chrome grill, gleaming hubcaps, pristine white sidewall tires and a red-and-white leather interior.

By itself, it would have been impressive enough. But even more astonishing was the sight of Brett, sitting in the driver's seat, his hands on the wheel. And beside him in the passenger seat was Mr. Crypinski—the same Mr. Crypinski who probably hadn't spoken more than a hundred words to her the entire time she'd known him—gesturing with actual animation while going on at length about his pride and joy's various attributes.

Rounding out the surreal tableau was Gavin. Perched on the edge of the back seat, the sleeves of his navy V-neck sweater pushed back to expose his forearms, which were resting atop the seat in front of him, he appeared engrossed, seeming to hang on the older man's every syllable.

It was…amazing. Unbelievable. More than a little wonderful.

And people don't believe in miracles, Colleen thought in bemusement. Apologizing for her fellow man, she sent a heartfelt word of thanks heavenward.

A second later, as if sensing her presence,

Gavin abruptly looked over and spotted her. ''Hey,'' he said. Although his voice was casual, something in the way his gaze played over her made her heart skip a beat and took the chill out of the night air.

''Hey, Ms. Barone,'' Brett echoed, doing his best to match Gavin's controlled cool, only to blow it with his next sentence. ''Isn't this *tight?*''

''Yes. It certainly is.''

''Mr. C's telling us all about it. Did you know that it can go from zero to sixty in under ten seconds? And that Elvis Presley owned one just like it?''

She shook her head. ''No. I didn't.''

''Well, he did. I can't believe you never told me about it.''

There was a faint note of accusation in the boy's voice, and Colleen realized it didn't have anything to do with Elvis, but about what he believed to be her failure to confide in him regarding the car's existence.

Before she could decide on the best way to respond, however, her landlord surprised her all over again, this time by coming to her defense.

"Now hold on," he said to Brett. "The truth is, she couldn't say anything to you because she didn't know anything." He sent Colleen an apologetic look, then turned back to face the boy. "I never thought to show her the car 'cause I just plain didn't think she'd be interested. This baby here—" he gave the T-Bird's glossy dash a fond pat "—well, it's kind of a guy thing. Or at least that's what Edna, my late wife, always said."

To Colleen's fascination, the other two "guys" immediately nodded and both knowingly murmured, "Ah," as if the older man's explanation was a perfectly acceptable defense for behaving like a male chauvinist.

She knew she ought to be offended, yet in this instance it just didn't seem that important. Not when it was so clear that the three of them were caught up in some serious male bonding.

That had to count for something, given that until she'd walked in here a minute ago she'd never in her life known three more stubbornly solitary individuals. Something very good indeed. And the last thing she wanted to do was put a damper on their good time. At least not tonight.

Not that she intended to roll over completely. Crossing her arms, she fixed her best expectant look on Brett, the one she'd worked hard to perfect during her tenure as a nun, and waited.

The boy managed to avoid her gaze for all of ten seconds, then finally looked over at her. "Sorry," he mumbled.

"Apology accepted. Did you get your homework done?"

He nodded.

"Good." Rubbing her hands down her arms, she manufactured a little shiver. "Now, I'm going inside. It's way too cold out here."

She turned and took a step, then stopped and looked over her shoulder. "Oh, I almost forgot. My mother sent one of her German-chocolate cakes home with me. You're all invited to come have a piece when you're done here."

With that she made her exit, wagering they wouldn't last outside another fifteen minutes.

As it turned out, she underestimated the lure of dessert.

They were at her door in under six.

* * *

Moira Barone might not be his favorite person, but Gavin had to give her credit.

The woman knew her way around a kitchen.

"Wonderful cake," he said to Colleen as he set his empty plate down on the coffee table in her living room. With a satisfied sigh he stretched out his legs and slouched down on his spine on the sofa.

"Are you sure you got enough?"

On the surface the question sounded sincere, but he was beginning to relearn the nuances of Colleen's personality, and one sideways look at the banked amusement in her eyes as she sat in the chair to his right, her bare feet curled beneath her, told its own story.

"Yeah. Three pieces was a bit of a challenge, but then, I like living on the edge." He'd also managed to outstay Emmett Crypinski and Brett, which had been his goal all along. For the usual male reason—the desire to get a particular woman into bed—he was in no hurry to leave. "So how was your dinner?"

She made a face. "Noisy."

"Any word yet on who's responsible for what happened Friday night?"

She shook her head. "No. Just a whole lot of opinions."

"Huh. Well, your family has certainly never lacked those."

To his gratification, the corners of her mouth tipped up. "Truer words were never spoken. But I'd suggest you try not to look quite so smug."

"And why is that?"

"Because as I was leaving tonight, Mother informed me she wants us to get together this week."

"Us who?" he said, suddenly wary.

"Who do you think? You and me and her and Papa. She said that unless she hears otherwise, she'll expect us for dinner this coming Thursday."

"Swell."

She sent him one of those mischievous smiles that always played hell with his insides. "Don't worry. I told her I couldn't possibly make a commitment without talking to you first. And as far as I'm concerned, we don't have to do anything just because Mother commands it. We can have dinner anytime. I'm thinking that February 2054 sounds about right.''

He couldn't help it, he laughed, his equilibrium restored, along with a curiosity about just what Colleen's mother had in mind. ''No, let's go. I can handle your mother.''

''Really?''

He nodded.

''Okay. If you're positive.''

''I am.''

''Now I have a question.''

''Shoot.''

''How did you ever wind up being so chummy with Mr. Crypinski?''

''Emmett?'' He shrugged. ''I don't know. He came by to fix your intercom, heard Brett and me discussing my Porsche, and out of the blue he got all bent out of shape, claiming there was no way some fancy foreign import could hold a candle to a real American car. That made Brett get on him, asking what made him such an expert, and the next thing I knew, we were on our way to his garage. And then once we actually clapped eyes on the T-Bird, things sort of snowballed from there.

''Brett asked him some question, and he

started going on about his baby's finer points, and…well, you heard them. It was like once they got started, neither one of them could shut up.''

"Amazing," she murmured. "Just a couple of weeks ago Mr. Crypinski wouldn't even let Brett into the house."

"Yeah, well, in this neighborhood it pays to be cautious."

"But tonight the two of them really seemed to be connecting," she said, disregarding his rather pointed remark.

Gavin considered the thoughtful look on her face and decided he'd let the other matter drop—for the moment. "I got the feeling that Emmett's lonely. And he said a few things that made it pretty clear he's been keeping tabs on Brett for a while."

"Really…" Her voice trailed off, and it was obvious from her arrested expression that something ingenious was going on in her mind.

He settled more deeply into the couch and found himself thinking, as one minute turned into two, that despite its well-used appearance, this particular piece of furniture was extremely comfortable. Which was more than he could say for the handsome taupe leather sofa that occupied his own living room at the Independence.

Which reminded him... "Colleen?"

"Hmm?"

"Tell me something."

"What?"

"Why *are* you living here? In a place like this?"

She looked over, focusing on him. "I'm not sure I know what you mean. It's my home."

He gazed steadily at her, letting his silence do the talking.

"Well, it is." She suddenly sounded just the slightest bit defensive. "Plus, it's close to school and shopping, which is convenient since I don't drive. And I like that I don't have to share space with lots of other people the way I would in a bigger apartment building."

He conceded the merits of her argument. "All right." Then he drove home *his* point. "But it's still Jefferson Heights."

"So? That happens to be where I'm employed. And in case it's somehow escaped

your notice, they don't exactly pay school social workers a ton of money."

Try as he might, he couldn't keep out the
edge that suddenly crept into his voice. "And
what? You're saving your trust fund for your
old age?" He knew damn well that each of
the Barone kids had received a million dollars
when they reached twenty-one. During the
time they'd been together he'd been acutely
aware of Colleen's upcoming windfall. And
his utter lack of one.

Yet to his surprise, rather than taking offense, Colleen suddenly laughed. "Oh, Gavin,
I'm sorry. I thought you knew. I gave it
away."

"You gave what away?"

"My trust money. Before I entered the convent, I signed it over to the Church to start a
scholarship fund for inner-city kids."

He felt his jaw sag and clamped it shut.
Still, he couldn't stop the shock shuddering
through him. "You gave away a million dollars?"

She nodded.

"Just like that?" He tried to take it in.

She shrugged one slim shoulder. "I didn't

need it," she said softly, a touch of sadness suddenly stark in her eyes. "I told you back when we were in college, remember? For me, my life, it's never been about money."

He sat back and stared at her.

Because ever since Friday night he'd been telling himself that what was between them was purely physical. That his sense of contentment the past two days was due to long overdue sexual satiation and because he and Brett really did seem to be connecting, as evidenced by their great time at last night's Celtics game.

He'd refused to ask any questions about— much less assign any significance to—his postcoital suspicion that Colleen had never been with any man but him.

And he certainly hadn't acknowledged that in just two weeks he'd come to feel more at home in her modest apartment than he ever had in his own swank penthouse—or anywhere else he'd ever lived.

But now...despite the wrong she'd done him in the past, he could no longer deny there was something special about her, something

hat drew him to her in a way that he'd never
been drawn to another woman.

But that wasn't all. There was also the fact
that even with him guarding himself against
her, in a ridiculously short period of time she'd
still managed to breach the substantial wall of
defense he'd built around his heart.

The wall she'd brought down once before,
only to abandon him, leaving him empty, de-
fenseless and hurting. The one he'd subse-
quently spent years fortifying and wasn't at all
certain he cared to surrender now.

The hell of it was, he realized as he stared
at her unguarded face, he wasn't certain he
had a choice in the matter anymore.

"Damn, Colleen," he said hoarsely. "What
are you trying to do to me?"

Seven

Colleen stared at Gavin's inexplicably grim expression. "I'm sorry, but I'm not sure... I don't understand what you're asking."

Abruptly he sighed. "Of course you don't. Oh, hell, I didn't mean..." He trailed off as if needing a moment to collect himself. When he spoke again, his voice was steady. "Do you trust me, Colleen?"

She felt a rush of relief, since the answer to that was easy. If there was one thing her years spent striving to do God's work had taught her, it was that when it came to putting one's faith in other people, the potential for reward was well worth the potential risk.

Besides, this was Gavin, whom she'd loved for such a very long time, and believed in even before that. "Yes."

He squeezed his eyes shut. "Thank God," he said softly.

She did her best to give him a few seconds before inquiring, "But why are you asking? What's the matter? Did I do something wrong?"

"No," he said instantly, opening his eyes. "It's me. If anyone screwed up, it was me." To her consternation, he rose to his feet and held out his hand. "Come here. Please."

Questions surfaced in her like weeds popping up in a garden after a good rain. Yet instinct told her it was somehow important that she stay silent and simply follow his lead. Taking his proffered hand, she stood and compliantly let him usher her out of the living room, down the hall and into her cozy but dark bedroom.

He reached over and switched on the table lamp.

Encircled by the resulting pool of light, they considered each other. It was so quiet the only sound was their not-entirely-steady breathing.

"Gavin—"

"Shh. Don't talk." He pressed a finger to her lips, then without warning toed off his shoes and shrugged out of his sweater and T-shirt. Her heart began to thump. "Friday night," he said quietly, tossing his clothes to the floor. "I thought... I was pretty preoccupied. It didn't occur to me that you'd never made love before. But you hadn't, had you?"

There was enough self-disgust in his voice that for a moment she was tempted to lie. Except that their gazes were locked and she knew she'd never pull it off. She shook her head. "No," she reluctantly admitted.

"That's what I thought."

"But it didn't matter," she protested. Surely he knew that she'd loved every moment of everything they'd done that night. "It *doesn't* matter. It was wonderful—"

"Yeah, it does matter," he contradicted, cutting her off. He undid the fly of his jeans, slid down the zipper and shucked off the rest of his clothes. "Because if I'd known, I'd have done things differently. For instance..."

He stepped so close that despite her clothes she could feel the heat radiating off him. Then he bent his head and began to lazily forge a link of kisses from her temple to her jaw. "I would've gone a whole lot slower." His tongue rimmed her ear, making her shiver. "I would've taken my time and made sure of your pleasure."

"Oh, but you did—"

"No. Maybe later. But not that first time." Deftly he unbuttoned her blouse and peeled it away, then managed to relieve her of the rest of her garments while also continuing the delicious torture he was inflicting with his mouth.

"I should've taken the time to tell you how much I love your breasts. The way they fit into my hands—" he cupped her "—the pale pink color of these—" his thumbs rubbed circles over her tightly beaded nipples "—the way they pucker at my touch."

"Oh, my gosh..." she said weakly.

"And then there's the way your waist curves in." His palms slid down her sides, his thumbs tracing her midline and the dip of her navel, gliding lower until only the tips of his little fingers rested against the lowest curve of her hips. "You're so damn delicate, Colleen. It turns me on."

"Gavin—"

He ignored her breathless little protest and feasted at the curve of her throat with his lips. Feeling as malleable as modeling clay, she let her head fall back to give him better access.

"So does the smoothness of your skin." His voice was a deep rasp abrading her nerve endings. "And how fast you get wet when I touch you here." With one finger he parted the dark curls between her thighs and stroked her.

She shuddered, her body feeling exquisitely overloaded. "Don't," she murmured weakly even though she was certain she'd die if he actually stopped now. "You shouldn't... I can't... It feels too... Oh, my, too..."

"Good?" he supplied. "I know, baby," he whispered, resting his damp forehead against her flushed skin. "Believe me, I know."

Even so, that didn't stop him from suddenly moving away.

"Gavin!" she wailed, her lashes fluttering up at the rude discovery that the only thing more excruciating than his teasing touch was the lack of it.

"Easy," he soothed, catching her by the wrist and drawing her with him as he backed toward the bed. "Hang on just a second. I promise you won't regret it."

His calves bumped against the side of the mattress and he sat. Then, before she completely understood what he intended, he was lifting her up. Laying back, he brought her down on him, impaling her on the silky thrust of his erection.

The sheer pleasure of it stole her breath.

But that didn't begin to compare with the joy that swept her as she looked down at his face. Because for a few seconds his expression was completely unguarded, allowing her to see the fierce tenderness, the intense emotion stamped on his features.

It gave her hope for the future. And the courage to follow her instincts.

Reaching down, she twined her fingers in

his, glorying in the strength of his powerful body. She met him halfway as he thrust upward into her, feeling herself getting lost in his gaze, feeling a compelling need to commit to memory every inch of his handsome, precious face.

Perfectly matched, they increased their pace. As they rocked together, their bodies coming together each time a little faster, a little harder, Colleen felt a rising pleasure that belonged to them alone.

Clamping down on her lower lip, she struggled to hold back, wanting to wait for him, wanting them to come together.

And then the moment came. With a strangled gasp he freed his hands and grasped her hips, pressing her down at the same time that his back hollowed and his body bucked. He surged upward, his whole body straining as he pumped himself into her, filling her with his seed.

Pleasure overtook her. Crying out, she gave herself up to the waves of sensation crashing through her. And finally gave voice to her heart.

"I love you," she whispered, tears of happiness filling her eyes as he locked his arms around her and cradled her close and she heard the reassuring thump of his heart against her ear. "I love you, Gavin. I always have. And I always will."

"I must say, I had no idea Elliot Sutherland once had a hotel in addition to the Independence," Colleen's father said before taking another sip of his after-dinner coffee. Setting the thin porcelain cup down on its platinum-ribbed saucer, he absentmindedly traced the outline of one of the finely embroidered flowers that adorned the Irish-linen tablecloth.

"And in Phoenix, of all places. But it certainly turned into a piece of luck for us that he did—and that he sent you to work there, Gavin. A pepper is the last thing I'd have suspected would be used to ruin gelato. Your experience and quick thinking helped save the day. If I failed to say it before, thank you."

"There's really no need, sir," Gavin replied, looking totally at ease as he lounged back in his chair at the long, burled-walnut table. "As the saying goes, I just happened to be in the right place at the right time—and the person to think of it first."

"You're being too modest, but I can see I'm making you uncomfortable, so we'll drop the subject for the moment. Why don't you tell me, instead, about this rumor I hear that you may be acquiring the old Commodore Hotel up on the North Shore?"

It was Gavin's turn to look impressed. "How did you learn about that? No one's supposed to know except my banker and my CFO."

"You get to be my age and you're bound to have a few inside sources," the older man said with a twinkle in his eye. "Although, if you don't mind a word of advice, you might suggest to your banker that he could use a more discreet assistant."

Gavin nodded. "You can bet I will. First thing tomorrow morning."

Listening with half an ear as the two men she cared for most in the world continued to talk business, Colleen wondered if it was possible to be too happy.

The past few days had been some of the most carefree and enjoyable of her life. The mentoring program, though still in its early stages, was going exceedingly well. And then, just yesterday, she'd had a very interesting talk with Mr. Crypinski regarding Brett.

There was also her ever-increasing closeness to Gavin, which figured heavily into her contentment. He'd spent every night at her place since Sunday, and though they were both on their best behavior and she knew that at some point they were going to have to address the hurt she sensed he still harbored regarding their past, in every other way their relationship was better now than it had been then.

And though she thought that was mainly because they were finally adults, she also had to admit there were times when her heart felt so childishly light it wouldn't have surprised her if it had taken flight like an untethered helium balloon.

Giving her arm a gentle squeeze, her sister Gina claimed her attention. Leaning close, she whispered, ''Congratulations. I was afraid that by dropping in unannounced—and as Mom made quite clear, uninvited—Joe and I were intruding on your big moment. But honestly, Colleen, I wouldn't miss this for the world.''

''What are you talking about?''

''You and your beautiful Irishman.'' She inclined her head at Gavin. ''It looks like Daddy likes him. And so does Mom, for that matter.''

Colleen involuntarily sneaked a quick glance at her mother and with a surge of relief saw that Gina seemed to be right. Moira was listening thoughtfully to the men's conversation, nodding from time to time when she agreed with something and appearing surprisingly content.

''As for the two of you,'' Gina went on, a rare teasing note entering her voice, ''you're a little scary. Every time you look at each other you glow like a pair of floodlights.''

Colleen bit down hard on her lower lip at the burst of laughter that wanted desperately to escape. Not until she was sure it was corralled did she turn her head to glance warningly at her sister. ''You little brat. Knock it off.''

''Why, Colleen Barone.'' The younger

woman did her best to look innocently bewildered. "Whatever are you talking about?"

"You know very well," Colleen admonished. "No more poetic images. Please. Not tonight."

"Oh, all right."

She returned her gaze to the men, but not before she caught her sister's laughter-laced whisper, "Spoilsport."

Her lips quivered so much that it was a moment before she could focus on the conversation. When she finally did, it was at almost the same instant that she sensed Gina coming to attention beside her.

"What did you just say, Dad?" Baronessa's VP of marketing and PR demanded to know.

Her father glanced over at her, his expression mild but unyielding at the same time. "Nothing you need to worry about, sweetheart. I was just remarking to Gavin that we could use a little help with public relations at the moment. And he was saying that he has a friend, a young man named Flint Kingman—" Carlo glanced at Gavin to confirm he had the name right, and Gavin inclined his head ''—who specializes in just this kind of corporate damage control.''

Joe, who was sitting across the table next to Gavin, nodded, ignoring Gina's suddenly stormy expression. ''I've heard of him,'' he said, addressing his remarks to the other two men. ''Doesn't he have a reputation of being a kind of a wonder boy when it comes to controlling the media?''

With an apologetic look at Gina, Gavin nodded. ''Yes, he does. In general he's very good at whatever he puts his mind to.''

''Perhaps you wouldn't mind, then, if I had my secretary call yours tomorrow for his phone number?'' Carlo inquired.

''By all means,'' Gavin said courteously.

With a gesture that was all the more ominous for its very deliberateness, Gina pushed away her plate and dropped her napkin beside it. With an impatient shove to her chair, she stood. ''Could I see you in the library, please, Father?''

With the faintest of sighs, Carlo nodded. ''Of course, Gina. If you'll excuse us?'' he said to the others.

Everyone nodded except Joe, who stood, instead. "Since this is about Baronessa business, I think I'll come, too, if it's all the same to you, Papa."

"Certainly." Looking just the slightest bit harried, Carlo quickly shook hands with Gavin and thanked him for coming to dinner, came around the table to give Colleen a buss on the cheek and whisper in her ear that he loved her, then marched in the direction of the library with his other two children in tow.

"Well," Moira, always the perfect hostess, said brightly into the sudden silence. "That was rather awkward, wasn't it? I do apologize for Gina's behavior, Gavin. Sometimes she can be very strong-willed. I must confess I simply don't understand from whom in the family she gets it."

"Yes, of course," Gavin murmured politely. He glanced at Colleen, then in quick succession at the door and his watch, his expression carefully neutral.

"Did I mention I have an early staff meeting, Mother?" Colleen said quickly. "We really should be go—"

"Oh, nonsense." Moira waved one elegant hand. "I haven't even served dessert yet."

"I'm sorry, but we really can't stay."

Moira hesitated the merest instant, then nodded graciously. "Very well. If you can't, you can't. But at least let your Mr. O'Sullivan finish his coffee. Surely you have time for that, darling?"

Colleen softened. As crazy as her mother sometimes made her, she knew the older woman's heart was in the right place; like most parents, Moira simply wanted what was best for her children—regardless if it was what *they* wanted. "Of course."

"Oh, good." Smiling, Moira turned up the charm, and the next ten minutes passed quickly.

Finally, however, Colleen motioned to Gavin and rose. "Thank you so much for having us, Mother," she said sincerely. "Dinner was wonderful, as always."

The three of them started toward the entry, stopping briefly at the hall closet so Gavin and Colleen could retrieve their coats.

"She's right, Mrs. Barone," Gavin said graciously. "If you ever decide you want a job, come see me. You'd be a draw in any of my kitchens.''

"Why, thank you, dear." Moira smiled, her beautiful eyes alight. "But I think I'd probably better stay around here. Although he'd never admit it, Carlo wouldn't last a day without me to look after him."

"His gain is my loss," Gavin said gallantly as they reached the front door.

Moira seemed to consider him for a moment, then reached out and gave him a pat on the shoulder. "I just want to say...I was wrong about you, Gavin."

Although his pleasant expression didn't change, Colleen didn't miss the thread of tension suddenly drawing him tight. "Were you?" he inquired politely. "In what way?"

"Despite your unfortunate background and all my dire predictions, you've grown up into a fine man, just as Colleen always claimed you would. I do hope you know it was never you personally that I objected to. It's just...Carlo always had such dreams about Colleen entering the religious life, and you both were so young. I hope you can see your way clear to understand that we simply wanted something different for our daughter.

"And really, I'm sure if you'll take a little time to reflect, you'll see that in some ways we did you a favor. After all, surely you wouldn't have felt nearly the drive to succeed that you obviously have if you'd married Colleen. And at least now you can honestly claim that the success you've had is your own."

Gavin's expression was so rigid by now that Colleen thought it was a miracle he could talk. "You're one hundred percent right about that, Mrs. Barone. Good night."

Assisting Colleen down the outside stairs with a hand to her shoulder, he walked tensely beside her to the Porsche, unlocked the passenger door and waited as she climbed in. Then he carefully shut the door, walked around the hood and slid into the driver's seat.

"Don't forget your seat belt," he gritted out as he locked his shoulder harness into place, turned on the ignition and pulled out.

He didn't say another word for a good ten blocks. Then he abruptly changed lanes and pulled off the main boulevard they'd been traveling and onto a residential street. Lips pursed, he scouted the area ahead, then pulled smoothly into the first open space at the curb.

Pulling on the parking brake with a jerk, he switched off the engine before finally turning to face her.

''Why, Colleen?'' he demanded. ''Why the hell have you let me think for all this time that you didn't love me enough to stick things out? Why the hell not just tell me it was your parents who objected all along?''

Eight

On some level, Colleen realized, she'd been waiting for Gavin to ask her this very question ever since he'd first approached her at Nick and Gail's reception.

Not that there'd been a logical reason for such an expectation. After all, she'd never told anyone about the afternoon all those years ago when she'd answered the imperious rap on her dormitory-room door and opened it to find her mother standing outside.

Just as she'd never repeated a word of their

subsequent conversation, the one that had pre-
cipitated her decision to end things with
Gavin.

Or shared how, once she'd finally stopped
crying hours later, she'd sat awake in the dark
the entire night, trying to plan exactly what she
was going to say to him, while doing her best
to anticipate his every argument and decide
how she'd counter it.

"So?" he said impatiently now. "Are you
just going to sit there? Or are you finally going
to have the decency to explain? You owe me
that, Colleen, at least."

He was right, of course. She squeezed her
eyes shut, asking the Almighty once more for
the wisdom to choose the right words. And
praying that whatever else happened, she
wouldn't hurt Gavin more than she already
had. Because if she did, she didn't think she
could bear it.

She took a deep, steadying breath. "First, I
want you to know that it's not fair to blame
my parents for what happened. Despite the impression Mother may have given you tonight,
ending things was my decision—and mine
alone."

"So what are you saying? That I should just forget everything she said tonight? That the truth is your mother couldn't wait to have me for a son-in-law?" He made a rude sound. "I don't think so."

"You're right. She didn't think we should be together, much less marry. But not for the reasons you think."

"Oh yeah? I can't wait to hear this."

She felt a prickle of irritation and did her best to ignore it. "When she came to see me, back while we were in college, she told me she'd heard we were dating...and that people were saying it was serious.

"And yes, Gavin, she was concerned. About me, but also about you. She said she'd known you since you were seventeen, and that no matter what I thought, I hadn't lived long enough to appreciate how hard your life had been—or understand how deep your pride ran. She feared that being with me would ultimately destroy you."

Gavin made another rude noise, but Colleen ignored it. "After all, she pointed out, I would have a million dollars. If we used it to live on, you'd be labeled a gold digger. But if I gave it away, you'd blame yourself for not being able to provide me with the kind of luxuries I'd grown up with. There was no way you could win."

"Right. So what you're saying is, you dumped me for my own good? Because you cared about me so much?"

"Yes! No! Darn it, Gavin, don't twist my words!"

"Me?" he shot back incredulously. "Listen, sweetheart, I'm not the one who pledged my undying love, then went off to become a nun. Or did you only do that to please your father?"

This time she felt a definite surge of temper. "Papa may have hoped I'd find my place in the religious life, but the last thing he ever wanted was for me to feel pressured or coerced. And I wasn't. By the time I fell in love with you, I'd been hearing God's call for a long while. I knew He had plans for me, I just wasn't sure what. And as it turned out, ultimately I made a mistake." One she'd paid for with hundreds and hundreds of hours of soul-searching and heartache and prayer.

"Yeah? Well, that makes two of us. Because while all this is fascinating, it still doesn't explain what's been going on the past few weeks. Or does it? Tell me, Colleen, what am I to you…really? Just another Barone-family charity project?''

She knew he was angry. But try as she might to tell herself that he didn't really mean what he was saying, his words cut to her heart. "Of course not," she flashed back. "But as long as we're on the subject, maybe I ought to ask you the same. Because while I know that I hurt you all those years ago, for which I'm truly, genuinely sorry, it's also true you didn't put up much of a fight to keep what we had. One bump in the road and you were gone so fast you practically left scorch marks on my carpet.''

He didn't give an inch. "At least I don't tell people I love them when I don't mean it.''

"I wouldn't know," she retorted, trying to keep the hurt out of her voice. "Since recently you haven't felt compelled to say those words to me. Which pretty much tells its own story, doesn't it?''

He didn't answer. Instead, looking straight ahead, he lapsed into a stony silence. Then he started the car and pulled onto the street. There was no mistaking the unyielding set of his jaw, which was perfectly visible every time they passed a streetlight.

Yet Colleen didn't care. All she knew after they'd traveled a few more blocks was that she found the silence unbearable. "Where are we going?" she demanded for lack of a better question.

Gavin gave a harsh, humorless laugh. "*We* aren't going anywhere. I'm taking you to your place. Then I'm going to the Independence. Where I belong."

She took one last stab at finding some kind of common ground. "If we could just talk rationally about this—"

"I don't think so, Colleen," he interrupted harshly. "Whatever's happened between us, now, in the past, whenever, it's over. You can bet the rent money on that."

Once again he turned his attention back to the road, not saying another word until they finally reached her place. Pulling to the curb, he reached over, shoved open her door and sat back. "Be sure and tell your mother thanks for dinner," he said with an edge of sarcasm that was razor-sharp.

He impatiently drummed his fingers against the steering wheel, looking less approachable than Mount Kilimanjaro in a blizzard.

While Colleen wasn't a quitter by nature, she realized she didn't have anything left to say. Her heart breaking, she did the only thing she could. Clinging desperately to what little was left of her composure, she climbed out of the car and forced herself to walk away.

She managed to make it all the way to the vestibule before the tears came.

Poised in the doorway of her office, which had in a previous incarnation served time as a broom closet, Colleen considered the piles of paperwork stacked in precarious towers on every possible horizontal surface.

If these files were lions and this was the Colosseum, I'd be the afternoon snack, she thought bleakly, not particularly surprised when even her minor attempt to amuse herself fell flat.

But then, in the week since she and Gavin had last spoken, that was pretty much the way everything had gone, she reflected, picking her way around the piles to reach her desk, which was actually an old closet door one of the janitors had thoughtfully placed atop a pair of two-drawer file cabinets.

In point of fact, it was actually a rather apt description of her life recently. As well as a fairly accurate picture of the state of her heart.

Both were flat. Utterly and completely without buoyancy. Bleak, humorless, leaden.

Goodbye, bright helium balloon. Hello, tasteless, wizened, hit-by-a-steamroller pancake.

But at least she was going to participate in one happy ending, she reminded herself as she sat down on the hard wooden seat of her creaky swivel chair. Reaching over, she plucked a file from the top of the nearest pile and set it carefully down in front of her.

Brett's name, in her own familiar handwriting, filled the index tab, and for the first time in days she felt an urge to smile.

Although it had taken some doing, she'd managed to hack through a jungle of red tape and get the Department of Child Services to sign off on a plan that would declare Brett an emancipated teenager and still provide him with a good, stable home while allowing him to spend regular time with his mother.

If he agreed—and the fact that it was his decision to make was the very best part, in Colleen's opinion—he'd have supervision, but not too much; he'd get to live with someone who genuinely cared about his future; and he wouldn't have to change schools or leave Jefferson Heights, both of which he'd repeatedly made clear to her mattered to him.

God Bless Emmett Crypinski, she thought a little mistily. Her gruff but secretly marshmallow-hearted landlord hadn't hesitated when she'd approached him with the idea.

Sure, why not? he'd said with one of his familiar shrugs. The kid wasn't really so bad, and he himself wasn't getting any younger. He wouldn't mind having someone around who could help out occasionally. And since she'd be just down the stairs, it wouldn't be as if he'd have sole responsibility for the boy, now would he?

All Colleen had left to do was sell Brett on the idea. Which shouldn't be that hard, not once she let it drop that Emmett had said it might not be a bad idea to teach the youngster to drive, as the Boston traffic was starting to be too much for a man his age.

With an amused shake of her head, Colleen took one last fond look at the worn file cover. Although she hadn't had to compile the usual caseworker studies or dozens of other documents in triplicate, since this was to be more a gentlemen's agreement between Emmett, Brett, herself and the State of Massachusetts, there were a few things she did want to clarify with Brett one more time, such as his birth date, his father's last known whereabouts, any phone numbers where his mother might be reached in case of an emergency.

Plus, it probably wouldn't hurt to toss out the notes she'd scribbled to herself the past few months as she'd pondered how best to see that the boy got the kind of future he deserved. Those sorts of things were always open to misinterpretation, so it would no doubt be best for everyone if they got filed in the garbage can.

Except that somebody had already beat her to it, she saw as she opened the manila folder.

Her heart, which had actually felt lighter for the past few minutes, sank like a stone. Because there was only one person she could think of who would've found the file contents of interest.

And that, unfortunately, was its main subject.

Gavin stepped briskly out of the elevator. With his head of security, James Maddux, bobbing along in his wake like a tin can tied to a bumper, he set off at a brisk pace down the carpeted corridor, trying hard not to lose his temper.

"At this point the last thing that concerns me is cost," he informed Maddux in no uncertain terms. "Just go ahead, have Lee Ellen in personnel set up the interviews and hire as many people as you think it's going to take. Our first priority—always—has to be guest safety.

"You know where I stand on this, Jamie. We've discussed it before. If our guests don't feel secure when they climb into bed at an O'Sullivan hotel, then none of the rest of it matters. Not our gourmet food, our beautiful accommodations or our first-class service. And I'm getting tired of having to repeat myself.

Almost as tired…'' Sweeping into the reception area that fronted the executive offices, he grabbed the sheaf of papers that Carol, his secretary, was holding out for him with one hand, while at the same time motioning her not to interrupt when he saw her part her lips to speak. "Not now," he murmured without breaking stride. "I'm making a point."

"But—"

He ignored her protest and picked up with Jamie. "As I said, I'm almost as tired of having to go over the same points again and again as I am of the whole damn place going to pieces every time I take a few mornings or afternoons off. So do your damn job, would you? Because that's why I'm paying you."

Satisfied that he'd made his point, he pushed open his office door and sailed inside.

Only to be brought up short as he saw a familiar figure standing at the windows, looking out. "Brett? What in blazes are you doing here?"

"I'm sorry, sir." Carol, appearing more than a little flustered, skidded to a stop beside him. "But I did try to warn you. First he showed up without an appointment, then he barged right in like he owned the place and insisted you wouldn't mind if he waited inside. Are the two of you related, by any chance?''

Gavin sent her a cutting look that had her beating a swift retreat, but not before she sent him a saccharine smile warning that, unlike the rest of the staff, she was done putting up with the foul mood he'd been unable to shake the past week.

''I'll hold your calls,'' she informed him in a dulcet tone of voice.

''You do that.'' He waited until he heard the door shut before he approached the youngster who continued to stare moodily out the window. ''What's up? Is something wrong? I didn't forget we had a lunch date, did I?''

Brett slowly shook his head. Shoving his hands into his pockets, he turned. ''Naw. I just came by to let you know I'm not going to be around for a while.''

''Ah.'' Clamping down on his escalating alarm, Gavin nodded, then walked over and sat down on the nearest of the two leather couches that formed one of several casual conversation areas in the big room. ''So.'' He stretched out his legs. "Where are you going?"

Brett shrugged. "I'm not sure, exactly. But somewhere for sure."

"Well, that sounds like a hell of a plan. You want to tell me what's going on?"

The kid remained silent, but just for another few seconds. Then he cracked, information spilling out of him like the yolk from a dropped egg. "It's Ms. Barone." Leaving his post at the window, he paced toward Gavin, anguish and anger mixed on his young face. "Man, I thought she was different! I thought I could trust her. But now—now I know she's just like all the others," he exclaimed.

Yeah? Well, I could've told you that, an ugly little voice in Gavin's head whispered.

Except when it came to Brett, she *did* care. Gavin knew it, with an utter, clear-down-to-the-bone certainty he didn't think to question. "What exactly did she do?" he asked carefully.

"I thought she was my friend," Brett responded bitterly. "I explained to her that I couldn't just take off, move across town or somewhere to live with a bunch of strangers and leave my mom here alone. As bad as things get sometimes, she still needs me to check up on her, to make sure she eats and has a place to live and stuff like that. And Ms. Barone, she seemed to get it.''

''So what did she do?'' Gavin repeated.

''She sold me out! I went into her office today, to talk to her about…stuff.'' For the first time the boy avoided Gavin's gaze, and with a slight shock Gavin realized that most likely the ''stuff'' the kid had wanted to discuss with Colleen was him. ''But she wasn't there.

''So I was waiting around, just hangin', when I knocked over this pile of papers, and there, right on top, was my file. And inside—'' Brett stopped, his young mouth trembling slightly before he regained control ''—inside there was this stuff about how smart I was, but I was too young to know what I wanted, much less needed, and then there was a list of phone numbers with the one for the State Foster Care coordinator circled and a note that said to be sure and give him a call, let him know that things were proceeding…'' He shook his head.

Gavin frowned. As tempted as he was just

to agree with the boy, to let his own feelings about Colleen take precedence over logic, there was something wrong here.

"Think about what you're saying," he said slowly. "Why would Ms. Barone go to all the trouble of putting together the mentoring program if she was secretly planning to send you off to who knows where? It doesn't make sense. Besides—" the next words came harder, for all that he knew in his gut they were true "—I don't think she'd do that. It's not Colleen's nature to betray people she cares about."

Hell, had he really said that? Did he mean it?

Telling himself firmly that this wasn't the time for such questions, he forced himself to concentrate on the issue at hand. "Plus, why would she think it would be best if you left the Heights? Not that it wouldn't be—" he sent the boy a look that effortlessly quelled Brett's instinctive protest "—but that's not the point.

"The point as far as you're concerned is that Colleen's made it her home. She really believes that as long as you try hard enough, good can come out of anywhere. Although where she came up with that particular piece of fantasy is anyone's guess.''

"Yeah, right." Brett gave him the sort of get-real look only a teenager could pull off. "That's easy enough. It's you. Even old Mr. C figured that out. He said something real sappy, like how he thought you were her inspiration for seeing to it that us kids got a fair shake. Or something like that.''

Gavin stared hard at the boy. No way, he told himself immediately, was he going to start putting stock in some kid's opinion. Much less that of an old codger like Crypinski.

After all, neither of them knew the whole, unvarnished truth. Not about his and Colleen's past. Much less about what had gone on between them these past few weeks.

And yet he couldn't entirely quell the sudden hope stirring to life inside him. Or stop himself from wondering… What if by some chance they were right?

He sank more deeply into the chair.

"Aw, hell," he murmured as he slowly began to look at the past few weeks from an entirely different perspective.

What in God's name had he done?

Even more importantly, if he could somehow drum up the guts, was there any way he could fix it?

Or had he already thrown away the best thing he'd ever had in his life for the second time?

Nine

"I'm so sorry, Mr. Crypinski." Swallowing hard because she absolutely was not going to cry, Colleen gazed fixedly through one of her living-room windows at the barren display of her garden outside. "This is all my fault. I didn't want to get up his hopes until I was sure I could make this thing with you happen, so I didn't take him into my confidence—not that I'm trying to make excuses. And now he's out there in the dark, all alone, and no doubt convinced I betrayed him."

Her landlord made a noise that sounded sus-piciously like what it was—an unimpressed snort. ''You've never been a ninny, Colleen, and now is not the time to start. Not only has Brett grown up on some of the toughest streets this city has to offer, but given his proclivity for dropping by here at all hours of the day and night, I can definitely assure you he's not afraid of the dark.

''As for the other, if he's got so little char-acter he'd assume the worst without giving you the benefit of the doubt, not to mention a chance to explain yourself, then the young fool deserves whatever happens to him. And as long we're talking plain, the same goes for that rich, hotshot boyfriend of yours who's suddenly MIA.''

She stared at the old man in amazement, so stunned by his uncharacteristic outburst she couldn't think what to say.

Not that he seemed to need prompting. ''That's how I see it, anyway. And don't think I haven't seen enough *Oprah* to know even an old guy like me is entitled to his opinion.''

''Yes, of course you are. I certainly didn't mean to imply...that is...'' Good heavens, she was practically stuttering, trapped between competing urges to laugh and cry.

Not that her companion appeared to notice. "You know what your problem is, missy? You're like my Edna, God rest her soul, too nice for your own darned good. You're always trying to take care of somebody, when maybe you ought to be letting that somebody take some care of you part of the time." Then his ears turned a fiery red as if he just realized how much he'd revealed. "Now if you'll excuse me, I need to check on my dinner."

"Yes. Of course." Trailing in his wake for no good reason except that she wasn't quite ready to be alone, Colleen followed him toward the door—only to practically leap a foot as the buzzer unexpectedly sounded.

Since he was closer by more than a yard, the building's owner reached out and pressed the intercom button. "Who is it?"

There was a lengthy pause, and then Brett's familiar voice said uncertainly, "Mr. C?"

"Well, it's not Santa Claus."

"Oh, thank you, God," Colleen murmured, her hand pressed to her heart.

"Sorry, Mr. C. I must've hit the wrong button. Will you let me in? I need to talk to Ms. Barone.''

"You're right about that," the older man retorted, hitting the release no more than half a second before he yanked open the apartment door and stepped into the hall. "And that's not the only person you're going to be doing some explaining to," he muttered.

Since Colleen's only thought at that moment was to make sure with her own eyes that Brett was all right, she followed him out into the corridor.

Only to take a step back as she caught sight of Gavin standing behind Brett like a silent shadow.

"Oh." She experienced a momentary sense of dislocation, as her emotions seemed to open ranks and split into two different camps.

Part of her was overwhelmed with relief that Brett was all right.

The other part was wholly focused on Gavin, drinking in the sight of him, examining his expression, his stance, the placement of each strand of his hair, doing everything it could to commit his image to memory.

To her dismay, Mr. Crypinski started down

the hall toward the entry, bearing down on Brett and leaving her feeling both alone and exposed. "It appears to me that you and I need to have a little talk."

With complete disregard for the teenager's yelp of objection, the former transit worker clamped his hand on the boy's shoulder, spun him around and began propelling him up the stairs toward his own second-story apartment.

Neither Gavin nor Colleen moved. Nor did they utter a sound.

Gavin, however, was having a field day berating himself. *She looks pale. And tired,* he thought, feeling as if an invisible hand were squeezing his heart. *And I'm an idiot.*

He took a step forward. "Hey."

She swallowed, her eyes looking big in her face as she stared at him. "Hey yourself."

"Are you okay? I mean, I suppose I should've called you when Brett showed up at the hotel, but it just sort of slipped my mind. I guess I thought it would be best all around if I simply drove him over." *Not to mention that it gave me an excuse to see you.*

"I'm fine. I just...I didn't expect...I guess I'm surprised to see you."

"Yeah, well, I don't blame you." He watched, frowning, as she hugged her arms to herself and rubbed her bare forearms with her palms. "You cold?"

The instant he said it he had a sudden desire to give himself a slap in the forehead. "Yes, of course you are," he answered himself, shrugging out of his coat as he advanced on her. "Here. Put this around you and let's get you the hell out of this drafty hall."

Despite the fierceness of his words, his hands were gentle as he wrapped her in his coat, then turned her around and herded her back into her apartment. "You really ought to hang a sweater on that wall rack by the door," he admonished, only to curse himself soundly when a quick sideways glance at her face as they awkwardly negotiated her narrow hall revealed that she was biting her lower lip to keep it from trembling.

"Colleen, *caraid*. Please. Stop looking so sad. I know I've been one hell of a giant fool, but I swear if you'll just give me one more chance, I'll spend the rest of my life making it up to you. Please, Colleen. As God is my witness, I love you. I always have and I always will, and all I'm asking for is some time to prove it.''

''You...you called me your darling,'' she said with a sort of wonder, turning toward him as they reached the relative warmth of her small living room.

''What?''

''*Caraid.* That's what it means.''

''Yeah, of course.'' He gave a little shrug, not about to admit that its precise meaning was news to him, that all he'd known for sure when he'd said it was that it was an endearment of some sort and the only fit-for-mixed-company Gaelic word in his vocabulary. Besides, whether he'd intended it to or not, it was exactly what she was to him. ''Just like I know how they spell the word for *stupid* in this particular neighborhood.''

A slight frown formed between her brows. ''Is it spelled differently here than in the rest of Boston?''

''Oh, yeah. Or maybe not. Beacon Hill or Southie, it's still spelled O-S-U-L-L-I-V-A-N.''

For the longest time, she gazed up at him, not saying anything, and then one corner of her mouth curved, just for a second. "Oh, Gavin, no. That isn't true—"

"Don't argue with me, Colleen. Only the world's biggest fool would let the only woman in the world meant for him almost get away not just once, but twice.

"I love you, Colleen. And I know we've got lots to discuss, lots to work out, but I don't want to spend another moment of my life without you. Make me the happiest man on the Eastern seaboard. Tell me you'll marry me."

Her face lit up, and then his coat slid in a heap to the floor as she raised her hands to cradle his face and he swept her into his arms. "Yes," she said fiercely, using quick kisses for punctuation. "Yes, yes, yes!"

But it wasn't until her mouth finally settled against his that Gavin knew everything was going to be all right.

There would be a lot to work out and discuss over the next days, weeks, months and years.

But as long as they had each other, he knew everything else would be all right.

*   *   *   *   *

DYNASTIES: THE BARONES

Marco Barone (d) m. Angelica Salvo (d)

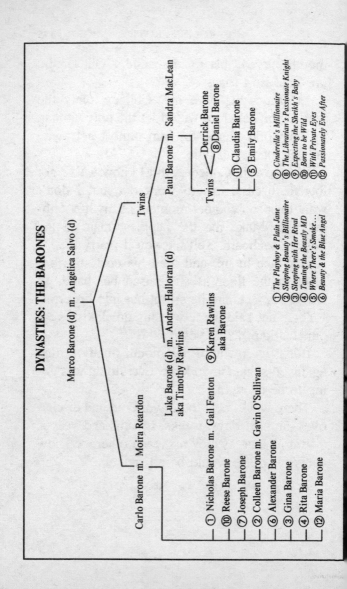

Carlo Barone m. Moira Reardon

Luke Barone (d) m. Andrea Halloran (d)   ⑨Karen Rawlins
aka Timothy Rawlins   aka Barone

Twins

Paul Barone m. Sandra MacLean

Derrick Barone
⑧Daniel Barone

Twins

⑪ Claudia Barone

⑤ Emily Barone

① Nicholas Barone m. Gail Fenton
⑩ Reese Barone
⑦ Joseph Barone
② Colleen Barone m. Gavin O'Sullivan
⑥ Alexander Barone
③ Gina Barone
④ Rita Barone
⑫ Maria Barone

① The Playboy & Plain Jane
② Sleeping Beauty's Billionaire
③ Sleeping with Her Rival
④ Taming the Beastly MD
⑤ Where There's Smoke...
⑥ Beauty & the Blue Angel

⑦ Cinderella's Millionaire
⑧ The Librarian's Passionate Knight
⑨ Expecting the Sheikh's Baby
⑩ Born to be Wild
⑪ With Private Eyes
⑫ Passionately Ever After

DYNASTIES: THE BARONES
continues....

*Turn the page for a bonus look
at what's in store for you in
the next Barones book—
only from Silhouette Desire!*

#1496 SLEEPING WITH HER RIVAL

*by Sheri WhiteFeather
February 2003*

One

Gina Barone wasn't in the mood to party, but she sipped a glass of chardonnay—praying it wouldn't irritate her stomach—and worked her way through the charity mixer, feigning an I'm-in-control smile.

She knew it was important to be seen, to hold her head high, especially now. Gina was the vice president of marketing and public relations for Baronessa Gelati, a family-owned Italian ice-cream empire—a company being shredded by the media.

Something Gina felt responsible for.

Moving through the crowd, she nodded to familiar faces. Although she'd come here to make her presence known, she thought it best to avoid lengthy conversations. A polite greeting was about all she could handle. And with that in mind, she would sample the food, sip a tiny bit of wine and then wait until an appropriate amount of time had elapsed before she said her goodbyes and made a gracious exit.

"Gina?"

She stopped to acknowledge Morgan Chancellor, a business associate who flitted around the social scene like a butterfly, fluttering from one partyer to the next.

Morgan batted her lashes, then leaned in close. "Do you know who asked about you?"

Gina suspected plenty of people were talking about her, about the fiasco she'd arranged last month, the Valentine's Day publicity event that had ended in disaster.

Baronessa had been launching a new flavor called passionfruit, offering a free tasting at their corporate headquarters. But pandemonium erupted when people tasted the gelato.

An unknown culprit had spiked the ice cream with a mouth-burning substance, which they'd soon discovered was habanero peppers—the hottest chillies in the world.

And worse yet, a friend of Gina's who'd stopped by the event at her invitation had suffered from an attack of anaphylaxis, a serious and rapid allergic reaction to the peppers.

She'd nearly killed someone. Inadvertently, maybe, but the shame and the guilt were still hers to bear.

Gina gazed at Morgan, forcing herself to smile. "So, who asked about me?"

"Flint Kingman."

Her smile cracked and fell. "He's here?"

"Yes. He asked me to point you out."

"Did he?" Gina glanced around the room. The crème de la crème of Boston society mingled freely, but somewhere, lurking amid black cocktail dresses and designer suits, was her newly acquired rival.

Anxious, she fingered the diamond-and-pearl choker around her neck, wishing she hadn't worn it. Flint's reputation strangled her like a noose.

The wonder boy. The renowned spin doctor. The prince of the PR world.

Her family expected her to work with him, to take his advice. Why couldn't they allow her the dignity of repairing the media damage on her own? Why did they have to force Flint Kingman on her?

He'd left a slew of messages at the office, insisting she return his calls. So finally she'd summoned the strength to do just that. But their professional conversation had turned heated, and she'd told him to go to hell.

And now he was here.

"Would you mind pointing him out to me?" she asked Morgan.

"Certainly." The redhead turned to glance over her shoulder, then frowned. "He was over there with that group of men, but he's gone now."

Gina shrugged, hoping to appear calm and refined—a far cry from the turmoil churning inside.

"I'm sure he'll catch up with me later," she said, wondering if he'd attended this party just to intimidate her.

If he didn't crawl out of the woodwork and

introduce himself, then he would probably continue to spy on her from afar, making her ulcer act up. It was a nervous condition she hid from her family.

"If you'll excuse me, Morgan, I'm going to check out the buffet."

"Go right ahead. If I see Flint, I'll let you know."

"Thanks." Gina headed to the buffet table to nibble daintily on party foods, to pretend she felt secure enough to eat in public. No way would she let Flint run her off, even if she wanted to dart out the door.

Balancing her food and a full glass of wine, she snuggled up to a floor-to-ceiling window, set her drink on a nearby planter ledge and turned to gaze at the city. Rain fell from the sky, and lights twinkled like pinwheels, casting sparks into the brisk March air.

She stood, with her plate in hand, admiring the rain-dampened view. And then she heard a man speak her name.

The low, vodka-on-the-rocks voice crept up her spine and sent her heartbeat racing. She recognized Flint Kingman's tone instantly.

Preparing to face him, she turned.

He gazed directly into her eyes, and she did her damnedest to maintain her composure.

She'd expected tall and handsome, but he was more than that. So much more.

In an Armani suit and Gucci loafers, he stood perfectly groomed, as cocky and debonair as his reputation. Yet beneath the Boston polish was an edge as hard as his name, as sharp and dangerous as the tip of a flint.

He exuded sexuality. Pure, raw, primal heat.

She steadied her plate with both hands to keep her food from spilling onto the floor. Men didn't make her nervous. But this one did.

He didn't speak; he just watched her from a pair of amber-flecked eyes.

"Aren't you going to introduce yourself?" she said, her posture stiff, her fingers suddenly numb.

A cynical smile tugged at the corner of his lips, and a strand of chocolate-brown hair fell rebelliously across his forehead.

"Nice try. But you know exactly who I am."

Like a self-assured predator, he moved a little closer, just enough to put his pheromones between them. She took a deep breath, and her stomach ignited into a red-hot flame.

Damn her nerves, she thought. And damn him.

"I'll stop by your office on Tuesday," he said. "At two."

"I'll check my calendar and get back to you," she countered.

"Tuesday at two. This isn't up for negotiation."

Gina bristled, hating Flint Kingman and everything he represented. "Are you always this pushy?"

"I'm aggressive, not pushy."

"You could have fooled me."

She lifted her chin a notch, and Flint studied the stubborn gesture. Gina Barone was a feminine force to be reckoned with—a long, elegant body, a mass of wavy brown hair swept into a chignon and eyes the color of violets.

A cold shoulder and a hot temper. He'd heard she was an ice princess. A woman much too defensive. A woman who competed with men. And now she would be competing with him.

*   *   *   *   *

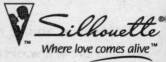

COMING NEXT MONTH

#1495 AMBER BY NIGHT—Sharon Sala
Amelia Beauchamp needed money, so she transformed herself from a plain-Jane librarian into a seductive siren named Amber and took a second job as a cocktail waitress. Then in walked irresistible Tyler Savage. The former Casanova wanted her as much as she wanted him, but Amelia was playing a dangerous game. Would Tyler still want her once he discovered her true identity?

#1496 SLEEPING WITH HER RIVAL—Sheri WhiteFeather
Dynasties: The Barones
After a sabotage incident left her family's company with a public-relations nightmare, Gina Barone was forced to work with hotshot PR consultant Flint Kingman. Flint decided a very public pretend affair was the perfect distraction. But the passion that exploded between Gina and heartbreakingly handsome Flint was all too real, and she found herself yearning to make their temporary arrangement last forever.

#1497 RENEGADE MILLIONAIRE—Kristi Gold
When sexy Dr. Rio Madrid learned lovely Joanna Blake was living in a slum, he did the gentlemanly thing and asked her to move in with him. But his feelings for her proved to be anything but gentlemanly—he wanted to kiss her senseless! However, Joanna wouldn't accept less than his whole heart, and he didn't know if he could give her that.

#1498 MAIL-ORDER PRINCE IN HER BED—Kathryn Jensen
Because of an office prank, shy Maria McPherson found herself being whisked away in a limousine by Antonio Boniface. But Antonio was not just any mail-order escort. He was a real prince—and when virginal Maria asked him to tutor her in the ways of love, Antonio eagerly agreed. But Maria yearned for a life with Antonio. Could she convince him to risk everything for love?

#1499 THE COWBOY CLAIMS HIS LADY—Meagan McKinney
Matched in Montana
Rancher Bruce Everett had sworn off women for good, so he was fit to be tied when stressed-out city girl Melynda Cray came to his ranch for a little rest and relaxation. Still, Melynda had a way about her that got under the stubborn cowboy's skin, and soon he was courting his lovely guest. But Melynda had been hurt before; could Bruce prove his love was rock solid?

#1500 TANGLED SHEETS, TANGLED LIES—Julie Hogan
Cole Travis vowed to find the son he hadn't known he had. His sleuthing led him to Jem—and Jem's adoptive mother, beguiling beauty Lauren Simpson. In order to find out for sure if the boy was his son, Cole posed as a handyman and offered his services to Lauren. But as Cole fell under Lauren's captivating spell…he just hoped their love would survive the truth.

SDCNM0203